Born in Greenock, Scotland, Jimmy Bain's early influences were those who walked a fine line between incorrigibility and the Strathclyde Police.

Always keen to give something back to society, Jimmy has been approached by the 'Friends of Barlinnie' for a donation from any royalties accruing from his three novels, *The Bumble's End, The Long Drop Goodbye* and *The Bumble on Beale Street* – failing to comply will hurt, they say – severely.

Married at Graceland, Jimmy counts The King as a close friend – though not one he sees often these days.

Coming soon from the same author:

The Long Drop Goodbye
The Bumble on Beale Street

More information at www.thebumble.co.uk

The Bumble's End

Jimmy Bain

With thanks to all the cats — BJ, Suzie and Gizzie — who've lent me a paw as I sat at the keyboard. Gratitude also to Visible Ink Writing Group in Edinburgh and to Ted and all members and staff of YouWriteOn. Oh, and to my wife, Barbara, for her assistance in putting this book together, amongst many many other things.

The Bumble's End is set in a time, not long ago, when smoking was encouraged everywhere.

Chapter 1

The last time I'd been in Edinburgh was in 1972 at the insistence of my father. He'd dragged me through to attend a July parade of the Orange Order. Banners flapped, drums and fifes played, sombre gents in bowler hats marched past in their dark suited Sunday best. Working class Protestants reminded working class Catholics of their place – even in a city with genteel aspirations.

No band played this time when I stepped off the Glasgow train. I strolled up from the hollow of Waverley Station and down towards Leith Walk, collar up and head down into a biting December wind that whipped in from the North Sea. Memories momentarily registered as I clocked the familiar Georgian buildings blackened by centuries of soot. Above, on Calton Hill, stood the phallic Royal Observatory tower, a white cross sitting atop. Next to it were the columns of the folly that resembled the Parthenon. Edinburgh – Athens of the North.

Half an hour later I was outside the address the Bumble had given me in Easter Road, a grimy run down area of the city with cheap shops and cheaper people. I was on a day out on a cheap day-ticket.

I scanned the illuminated names behind the Perspex cover at the side of the door. There was no point in alerting anyone up there to my presence, so I pressed other buttons in the hope I could gain entry. I amused myself imagining people cursing because they'd just stepped into the bath, picked up their favourite read, or were about to get intimate.

A female voice answered from the third button I tried. 'Hello?'

'Department of Social Security,' I said. 'Trying to contact one of your neighbours, a Mr Charles Manson.' It was the best I could come up with at the time.

'I don't know him,' she replied.

You wouldn't want to, I thought. She buzzed the door release mechanism though, and I made my way up the dim stairwell, past torn black rubbish bags and several bicycles chained to the banister. No one came out to challenge me. I stopped outside the door marked *Cowan* on the fourth floor. Short of breaking it down there wasn't much option but to press the bell. What the heck, I thought. As I reached for the doorbell, I realised I didn't need to ring, as the door was slightly open. A black cat wandered out, sniffed the air and rubbed itself against my leg. My luck was in. I shouted a *Hello* though, in case there was a dog waiting inside to chew my bollocks off, but there was nothing, not a sound.

I stepped in cautiously. The flat was dingy and unlit, so I felt around for the light switch and flicked it on. The bright glow revealed a dismal choice of decor. The hall wallpaper was pink and red striped; the carpet mottled green with a swirl of autumnal browns. A solitary picture of a white-robed Jesus, giving the peace sign, stared back from a calendar on the left hand wall. A warm sweet sickly odour pervaded the place and made you immediately want to take a shower. Something was dead, of that there was no doubt.

I followed my nose to the second door on the right and half turned before going in. There wasn't anyone watching me except Jesus. I pushed the door. It wouldn't move and I had to put my full weight behind it to create a gap big enough to squeeze through. Even though it was early afternoon the room was dark. I could just make out the outline of a body propped up against the back of the door, its legs splayed out on the carpet. I tried the light switch a couple of times but the bulb had blown, so I made my way to the window and threw the curtains back. Several pigeons took off from the window ledge. I turned back and looked at the body.

It was Tony McCaffrey, the Bumble's nephew. I recognised him from the photo I'd been given.

There was a rope around his neck, which hung from the brass coat hook, and his backside was suspended a couple of inches off the floor. His tongue bulged from his mouth as though someone had stuffed it there, like an apple in the fatted pig. His rigid arms were outstretched as though he was about to welcome me, while his long dark hair had fallen over his face. His only item of clothing was the gold crucifix around his neck with the Man nailed to it. Again I was looking at Christ and he was looking back at me.

I prised open the window to let some fresh air into the room, then sat on the edge of the unmade double bed and lit a cigarette. I surveyed the scene while the pigeons settled back down on the ledge. One of them had a stump for a leg and I wondered what had happened. In America some country singer would write a song about it. *On a wing and a prayer with Pigeon Pete, only one leg so hence no feet* – or words to that effect.

I snapped the Zippo shut, took another draw on my cig and looked Tony over. I felt his face. He was cold as the proverbial marble. I reckoned he had been dead a day or so. It was then I noticed the deep bruising on his wrists and ankles. He had been bound at some stage prior to death. I couldn't help but look again at the crucifix. The pigeons began to coo as they became amorous on the windowsill.

Well, I had finished my job. But I was still none the wiser as to why the Bumble wanted his nephew found. My instructions were clear – persuade him to return to Glasgow. That would no longer be a problem, he'd be going as a VIP in a long black limousine.

I stepped over the body and looked out of the back window. There was nothing to recommend the garden. It was a bleak wilderness with a solitary shopping trolley lying on its side. Stumpy the pigeon was oblivious to me, as his love interest circled about on the ledge. He makes a remarkable job of staying upright, I thought, for a one-legged randy pigeon. I took a few more draws and flicked my cig out the window and turned to see I wasn't alone.

He was older than I remembered, but I knew who he was the moment I saw him. He still had a mop top of red curly hair, his face framed by black NHS spectacles with lenses as thick as the bottom of milk bottles. It was Jim Cowan, the Bumble's brother. We stood looking at each other and then at Tony McCaffrey.

'Is he...?'

'Yeah, he's dead Jim. You could stick a pole up his arse and windsurf him down the Clyde.' I opened my packet of Marlboros and offered them towards him.

'I gave up,' he said, taking one.

Yeah, you and me both, I thought and struck my lighter.

He coughed on the cigarette. 'Is there anything we can do for him?'

I shook my head. 'No. But a blanket to cover him over would give him a bit of dignity.'

He nodded approval as I pulled off one of the grubby sheets from the bed, and covered Tony over.

'You're going to have to call the law, Jim,' I said. 'Tony here didn't die from natural causes.'

'No shit,' he said and we both gave nervous smiles. 'What are you doing here anyhow?' he went on.

I picked a piece of tobacco from the tip of my tongue. 'The Bumble offered me a job to find Tony here.'

He looked puzzled. 'But Tony was never lost. Said he wanted to come through and party in Edinburgh for a few days, that's all.' He coughed some more on the cigarette. 'He frequently got into bother in Glasgow... you know how it is.' He looked down at his nephew with sadness in his eyes and sighed. 'His mother'll be upset.'

No kidding, I thought and took a draw on my cig. 'Mind telling me where you've been?'

'You think *I* would...? I've been away for a few days that's all. Christ! You really think I'd kill Tony? Like that? Maybe you killed him!'

'Wise up,' I said. 'He's solid enough to break with a hammer. Where have you been? The police will want to know.'

'I was at a works conference in Aberdeen. Been there the last two days. Dozens of people can vouch for me.'

We both flinched at the crash of heavy feet on the stairwell. I peered out of the front window at the street but couldn't see any Plods or their cars. My instinct told me things were going to get worse before they got better. A few seconds later I heard the flat door being pushed open and then the sound of male voices. I also detected animalistic pants and slobbering. Jim Cowan backed away from the door and joined me at the window. I half expected him to jump up into my arms as an ugly face with a chain attached to it came around the door. The dog didn't look much better either.

It was Kev Barr. Tony's corpse got ploughed to the side as he shoved his way through and stood there big and ugly in a full-length brown leather coat. A shaved head added to the persona. He resembled Marlon Brando – not like when he starred in *The Wild Ones*, but latterly – a fat bastard. Behind him stood a guy with a dark goatee beard and gold earring. He wore a combat jacket and was carrying a baseball bat. The day out was becoming something to write home about.

Kev's mutt showed an interest in the deceased. 'What have we got here then, Tango?' He threw back the sheet covering Tony. The dog instantly sniffed at the corpse's nether regions. Hanging has the habit of loosening the bowels.

'Well, well if it's not Tony McCaffrey! What a surprise. Fancy finding him hanging around here.' Kev laughed, loudly and Tango barked as though in approval at the joke. 'Didn't expect the pleasure of your company.' He looked up and smiled towards me, revealing an upper row of pure white teeth that had spent the night in a jar of Sterodent.

I flicked my finished cigarette past his ear. 'Too bad you couldn't have been permanently detained at Her Majesty's pleasure in Barlinnie.' The smile on his face vanished.

'You're a bit out of your swamp,' I went on, 'coming through here.'

'I've expanded. My organisation even has a cultural exchange programme these days. Meet Trotsky here, he's a Moscow lad.' He turned and gave a thumb up sign to his Slavic minder as though he was the magician's assistant. The Russian's expression didn't change. He didn't haul anybody by the ears from a top hat.

Kev paused and looked down at Tony again, almost with a hint of compassion, while Tango licked the deceased on the cheek. 'He disappointed me, did Tony. He was bright, had a future, but then he tried to get smart. Thought he'd hold out on us, just like that bastard of an uncle of his, the Bumble.'

'So you hanged him?' I said.

He laughed with menace and Tango once more barked approval. 'Naw, not me.' He studied the corpse. 'I leave that to Trotsky here, one of his favourite methods... a trick he picked up in Afghanistan.'

It was time to apply the first rule of negotiation. 'What the fuck do you want Kev?'

He shrugged his shoulders. 'Tony took something that doesn't belong to him. I want to have a look round.'

'I don't think so,' I said, with a shake of my head. 'But then, it's up to Jim here. It's his place.'

'You taking the pish?' Kev unbuttoned his coat to reveal a sawn-off shotgun tucked into a custom made carrying pouch. He pulled the snuffling Tango away from Tony McCaffrey and pointed him in the direction of Jim Cowan. The dog gave a low growl.

Just then there was a loud meow from the hallway. Tango, sensing the pleasure of cat on a stick, pulled round sharply, catching Kev off guard. Kev fell over and landed on top of the

11

corpse. The body farted loudly as the gases in the stomach were expelled.

'Jezus fucking Christ!' Kev was still attached to Tango by the chain around his wrist. He writhed on the floor and screamed in agony as 170lbs of Rottweiler attempted to haul him round the door in pursuit of feline fare. Somehow he managed to break free and Tango launched off after the cat, barking. I heard shouting as someone came out of a flat to investigate the commotion.

Tango's actions also caught the Russian off guard and I shouted to Jim Cowan to run for it. I wasn't quite quick enough to get past him myself and he swung the baseball bat at my head. He missed. I stepped forward to take a punch at him and tripped on the hall rug, my head clipping the table as I went down.

There was a split second when everything went into freeze-frame and the voices faded. My eyes focused on the white-robed Christ in the hall as I attempted to get to my knees and I heard myself, again, telling Jim Cowan to run for it. Then everything went blank.

When I came to, I was on the floor trying to make sense of where I was. My head was pounding. Easing myself up, I made sure the front door was closed. I had to steady myself for a moment before I went to find the bathroom. After running the cold tap for a minute or so, I dipped a hand towel under the flow then applied it to my temple. A pale face with several days' dark growth looked back from the mirror. I was also available for hauntings.

There wasn't a sound – nothing. I half expected to find myself on the end of a rope like Tony McCaffrey or being savaged by Kev Barr's dog, but no, they must have legged it. I called out for Jim Cowan but he didn't reply.

I searched the rooms. The deceased revealed nothing. On the windowsill, Stumpy the pigeon was still trying to get his end away. The room was now cold, so I closed the window. Sitting down on the bed, I lit a cigarette and felt the lump on the side of my head.

Besides a dead Tony McCaffrey, I now had a missing person in the shape of Jim Cowan. I got up and looked around a bit more. I went through the flat from one end to the other but nothing seemed out of place. It was a bachelor's pad – no sense of femininity anywhere. The toilet seat remained upright at all times.

Jim's bedroom was full of old fashioned furniture in dark brown wood, solid and functional. I searched the bedside cabinet but found little beyond a copy of the gay magazine, *Pride,* and a bottle of Paracetamol. Maybe being gay was a king sized headache. There were a number of adverts ringed in the lonely-hearts section. I searched the closet but Jim definitely wasn't in it. I put the magazine back and went into the kitchen. It was tidy. The cupboards contained nothing but tinned food and storage jars and a selection of cereals. I found an old newspaper, spread it on the kitchen floor and emptied the contents from the jars on to it. I poked through the food assortments with a fork – nothing. Hell, I even opened the tins – still nothing.

I looked in the obvious places like under the rugs and down the backs of the settees. Even the cistern in the toilet – but I still drew blanks. The only location left was the other bedroom – the one Tony occupied.

I put the sheet back over him and hoped the bed bugs didn't object to cold fodder. There was an old oak chest of drawers in the corner of the room and I began to empty it systematically. The top drawer contained nothing but socks, Y-fronts and T-shirts. The middle drawer produced little to fire the imagination beyond a large black vibrator that needed new batteries. But the final drawer did produce something out of the ordinary, amid the adult magazines and videos.

Tucked inside *Bondage Babes* was a small dark green book that looked a bit like a passport, and some letters. The book had few pages and contained nothing beyond wartime dates, with an official stamp of a coat of arms beside them. A black and white photograph of a couple posing under a tree was inside it. He was young, dark and solemn, with deep-set brooding eyes covered by a single eyebrow – he was also wearing a wartime German uniform. The woman was younger and looked up at him as though she thought she'd made a good catch. He must have had charm, power or money to attract her. There was nothing on the back of the photo to indicate who they were.

I flicked through some more magazines. They offered everything from rubber-hooded fetishists to correctional therapists willing to flail your arse off. I looked over at Tony and went, *tut, tut, tut.* Then I noticed a small cloth badge had fallen on the carpet. I picked it up. It was a stylised embroidered eagle – a Nazi eagle clutching a swastika. It was finely made with gold wire and must have adorned a dress uniform. I frowned. I hadn't figured Tony for a militaria collector, or for a Neo-Nazi. Pocketing the mystery items, I thought I'd better put the rest back in the drawers – but when I looked at Tony, I decided not to bother.

14

My thoughts returned to Jim Cowan. If he had legged it and raised the alarm, the place would surely be crawling with police by now. Still, I reckoned Jim had to have been taken by Kev and the Russian. I didn't think there was any point in calling the law myself right now – a naked dead man on the end of a rope along with a missing gay man wouldn't go down well with the police. No. Tony was dead, and for the moment was unavailable for comment.

The other thought going through my head was how I was going to break the news to the Bumble. I found the phone in the hall and figured there was no time like the present. Picking it up, I slumped to the floor feeling light headed, lit a cigarette and dialled his number.

Just then the theme tune from the *Lone Ranger* echoed from a door chime box above my head. I froze and put the receiver down. I looked up at the picture of Jesus on the wall and we exchanged glances. He said, *It's your call man,* so I stood up, and peered through the spyhole in the front door. There were two of them, guys, clean cut and wearing dark raincoats. I stood back from the door and took another draw on my cig. They pressed the doorbell again and the full rendition of the *Lone Ranger* theme galloped out from above the door.

Who the fuck were they? They were too smart for any of Kev Barr's mob – or for the CID. Once again the theme tune started up. That was fucking it! Corpse or not, I'd had enough of this. I yanked the door open and couldn't care less if Tonto, Kimo Sabi and fucking Silver were out on the landing.

'Yeah? What the fuck you want?'

'Good afternoon sir, we are from the Church of Christ of the Latter Day Saints,' the tall one said in an American accent.

They were fucking Mormons.

'I'm brother Harringdale and this is my colleague, brother Mulvey. We're here to tell you that there is hope beyond death if you believe in the Lord.'

I just stared at them, wondering which one I would punch first.

'Could we...?'

I didn't hear the end of his sentence as I slammed the door in their faces. I swear the picture of Jesus was smiling – a sly mocking smile – especially when they put a leaflet through the letter box.

I sat back down on the floor and once again picked up the phone to dial the Bumble. It rang a couple of times and then I heard the polite Glaswegian tone that he put on for punters.

'Cowan Investigations, how may I be of service?'

'It's me,' I said. 'Don't say anything just listen. I've got a result for you.'

'A result? You've talked to Tony?'

'No, you're going to need a medium for that.'

'A medium?'

'Yeah, they communicate with the dead, Davie.'

There was silence for a few seconds.

'Where are you?' he asked.

'I'm at your brother's flat on Easter Road.'

'Is Jim there with you?'

'No,' I said, 'he's vanished. Listen, it isn't wise to discuss this on the phone. Come through and meet me at the bar in Waverley Station, and call the Chinaman and have him meet us there as well, we need some information. I'll tell you all when I see you.'

'Right,' he said and the line went dead.

I put the phone back on the hall table and went into the kitchen. I found a yellow duster and a can of Mr Sheen spring fragrance and began to clean the surfaces I had touched. When I finished, I picked up the leaflet from the doorway and looked at it. 'Arise with Christ!' it exclaimed. I left it beside Tony McCaffrey.

Zipping up my jacket, I opened the front door, stepped out and closed it behind me. Then I pressed the doorbell.

Hi ho fucking Silver!

Chapter 2

I stepped out onto Easter Road. The sky was a luminous grey with the odd swirl of pink. God had his artist's head on today. I thought of hailing a cab but decided to leg it back towards the city centre sharpish. I needed to avoid being clocked by any possible witness who might remember me.

A Salvation Army brass band knocked out *Oh Come All Ye Faithful* as I fought my way past the Christmas shoppers at the east end of Princes Street. I went down the Waverley steps and into the station. A young guy with a forlorn look and a wispy growth on his chin waved a magazine in front of my face. 'Big Issue? Help the homeless – special Christmas edition.' A large mongrel sat faithfully beside him wearing a red Santa hat.

I fumbled in my pocket and handed him a tenner. 'Keep the magazine mate,' I said, 'nothing personal.'

I shoved my way past a young couple who only had eyes for each other, and into the inner arched quadrangle of the Railway Bar. The Chinaman was already there. He nursed a glass of scotch at a table in the corner, along with a couple of sad bastards who looked as though they had no intention of catching a train. Though by the look of them they'd had their tickets well punched.

The Chinaman's real name was Reuben McKenzie. He'd been a newspaper hack in Glasgow with the Daily Record and moved to Edinburgh after he'd got into an affray with a hoodlum over an exposé about cocaine and an underage sex racket. The encounter resulted in Reuben being stabbed and losing a lung. Hence 'Wun Lung, the Chinaman'. He'd been working for the Bumble as well – having supplied me with the recent mug shot of Tony.

He still had the same hawkish features and a swarthy complexion complemented by a dark beard. I remember him claiming once that his looks came from shipwrecked Spanish sailors from the Armada who had shagged the local fluff up in the Western Isles. Well, it must have made a change from the sheep.

I nodded to him; he indicated his half pint glass and held up his whisky chaser that needed a refill. I went to the counter.

'Half a lager,' I said to a ruddy-faced barman who looked as though he had been dookin for apples in the chip pan.

'McEwans or Becks?'

I wasn't sure if the Chinaman was partial to piss so I ordered Becks and two large whiskies. I navigated past a several travellers with cases and pulled up a chair beside Reuben. 'Thought you came to meet me.' I gave the two scruffy unshaven characters in conversation next to him the once over. 'Can we lose the great unwashed?'

'Shh... Contacts laddy,' he said and reached for the whisky. 'Name of the game. You'll hurt their feelings. This is their local. They're my eyes and ears – you'd be amazed at what goes on in here.' He made a V with his index and middle fingers, pointed to his eyes and then made a level sweep of the bar with his hand like some Shaman.

'Lose them, Reuben. Go tell them to prop up the bar.'

'They'd probably appreciate an incentive.'

I sighed and handed over a twenty note.

'You're a gentleman,' said the Chinaman.

'Yeah, yeah, just tell them not to hurry back.'

He quietly conveyed that we wished to be alone. His flea-bitten buddies were more than happy to make themselves scarce. Reuben moved his chair closer to myself. Taking the whisky, he raised his glass in mock salute. 'Cheers.'

I didn't bother with small talk about what we'd both being doing since we last saw each other. 'Any idea why the Bumble wants Tony?' I said.

'What's up?' he asked, lowering his glass.

'Just tell me anything you know about his nephew,' I said, 'and don't give me any old tosh.' The Chinaman hesitated. I glanced at my watch. 'You've not got much time, if the Bumble's moved his lardy arse, he should be here shortly.'

'Okay, okay, rumour has it, it's personal between him and the Bumble, but beyond that I have'nae a clue. He paid me to follow Tony about for the last few days, nothing more.'

I unzipped the top pocket of my leather jacket, fished out my packet of Marlboros and offered him one. Despite his half capacity for inhaling he accepted. I fired up my lighter, 'With the Bumble there's *always* something more.' I snapped it shut.

I passed the Chinaman the photograph the Bumble had given me. He glanced at it.

'Who's the fucker beside Tony?' I said stabbing at the figures with my index finger. 'And don't shrug your shoulders and say you don't know – you took it.'

The Chinaman sighed, gave the bar a hundred and eighty and leaned forward.

'He's a Russian and part owner of a nightclub in the city – the Pink Angel. Rumour has it that he allows Kev Barr to trade there with his assortment of mind altering substances... you know, Kev Barr, your old pal, the Mr Big of spice and vice. You do know he's out of the nick?'

'Yeah, I know. Had a less than cordial meeting with him and that guy in the photograph a couple of hours ago.'

'Jeezus.' The Chinaman paused mid-inhalation. 'What about Tony – was he there too?'

'Yeah,' I said taking a deep draw, 'he was hanging on the back of a door with a rope around his neck.'

'Jeezus!' he said again and downed his whisky. 'Is he...?'

'Yeah, he's dead.'

The Chinaman crossed himself Catholic style.

There was silence for a moment. A female announcer informed waiting passengers over the tannoy that the Aberdeen express was running approximately forty minutes late due to severe weather further north.

'I'll get us another drink,' said the Chinaman.

I nodded.

Several minutes later he placed down a couple of glasses.

'So where did you take this photograph?' I said stubbing out my cigarette in a glass ashtray.

The Chinaman sipped his drink. 'Outside the Pink Angel.'

I raised my eyebrows. 'Is the joint exclusive?'

'In that it's gay? No, I understand straights are occasionally allowed in.' His eyes tracked somebody behind me. 'The cavalry has arrived.'

I turned to see my employer, former Detective Inspector Davie Cowan, aka the Bumble, squeezing his tractor size spare tire past a couple of punters with shopping bags. He ran his hand through his thinning red hair while his piggy brown eyes fixed me to my seat. A half smoked cigarette hung from the corner of his mouth.

He sat down. 'Spill it.'

'You might want a drink,' I said.

'Fuck the whisky – give me a report!'

I told him everything that happened, except for the matter of finding the Nazi items.

'Christ Almighty!' he said. 'Whit the fuck am I going to tell his mother?'

'Nothing. The cops will suspect something if her reaction to the news shows she already knows.' I slipped the Chinaman a ten pound note and glanced in the direction of the bar.

'I've just been to get the bloody drinks.'

'Well go again,' I said. 'They bang on about the Scots being unhealthy bastards, the exercise will do you good.'

He pushed his chair backward scraping it along the tiled floor and snatched the note from my hand.

'You're sure he was dead?' said the Bumble forcefully extinguishing the life from his cigarette.

'As the Dodo,' I said.

'Fuck.' The Bumble lit another cig. 'Fucking Kev Barr, they should have kept him locked up.'

A few minutes later the Chinaman returned with drinks. The announcer informed the station that the Aberdeen train was now running an hour late.

The Bumble downed the contents of his glass in one and handed the empty glass back to the Chinaman. 'I need another one, make it large this time.'

'I've just got the bloody round,' he protested.

'Well get another one!' said the Bumble. 'Christ! What the hell do I pay you for?'

I nodded to the Chinaman to be obliging.

The Bumble waited till he was out of earshot. 'Look – stay on the case – and don't inform the police.'

I looked directly at him, 'I don't think that's a wise move. It might be better if you drop by your brother's flat and accidentally discover Tony – say you were just visiting, you know, doing the family thing at Christmas. That way you can inform the police and then Linda.' I lit another cig and watched a smoke ring float towards the heavens. 'But as for working for you on a murder, especially within your family...well, I'm not sure, not sure at all.'

A businessman at the next table lowered his newspaper and pretended to pick a piece of lint from his black Crombie overcoat. He watched the Bumble grab my arm and plead. 'Please – for old times sake.' I stared back at the gent. He resumed interest in reading The Scotsman.

'There's something you're not telling me,' I said as the Chinaman returned with re-fills.

'Later,' said the Bumble. He knocked back the whisky and winced. 'I've tasted better methylated spirits. This the cheap stuff you got?'

'That's gratitude for you,' said the Chinaman.

I turned to the Bumble, 'Well, if I'm still on the case I'll need to find a place to stay.'

He smiled and put a hand on my shoulder. 'You won't regret this.'

'I already have,' I felt the lump on the side of my head. My instinct told me to walk round to the booking office and buy a one-way ticket back to Glasgow and to hell with Edinburgh.

But I felt bad about what I'd found and Jim Cowan might need all the help he could get.

'You should crash at mine,' the Chinaman said.

'Thanks Reuben, but this matter might get a bit hairy and you're running on half capacity as it is – no offence.' I didn't trust him an inch. 'Maybe you could recommend a bed and breakfast nearby?'

The Bumble glanced at his watch. 'Right, I'll get a taxi down to the flat and call the law when I get there. Gae us a ring tonight, doesn't matter what time and here's five hundred to keep you going.' He slid a plain brown envelope across the table. I studied it for a moment, then shoved it into my inside pocket. The Bumble stood up. 'Thanks,' he said and headed towards the exit. It had turned into the season of goodwill.

I turned towards the Chinaman. 'Fancy a date at the Pink Angel then?'

'You asking me out?'

'Strictly on a professional basis,' I said. 'I'll pay for your time.'

'You talk my language. You've got my number?'

I nodded. He recommended a B&B a few streets along from his own pad.

'Okay,' I said, 'I'll call you later I'm going to grab a dogburger and fries over there at the fast food emporium. You sure you want in on this?'

'It sells newspapers and pays my rent,' he said, 'catch you later.'

I caught a taxi to the Craigside boarding house in the respectable west end of the town and rang the doorbell of a traditional Edwardian villa. Coloured bulbs flickered on a small fir tree by the steps that swayed in the easterly wind.

A white-haired old man with a hangdog expression appeared. I checked out his black and yellow striped waistcoat and said, 'Got a single room pops?'

'Should have.' He shuffled back into the hallway while a small yappy tan dog with a red tartan ribbon attached to its head defiantly barked at me. I stepped inside. It barked some more. The old guy searched about behind a wooden counter, produced a set of keys with a large brass doorknob attached to them and handed them to me. Handy, I thought, if things get rough.

'Sign the Register please. Room 8, top of the stairs... breakfast is between 7 and 8:30 just down those stairs.' He jerked his thumb in their direction.

An elderly woman appeared from an alcove behind him and scooped up the dog. 'Would you like an evening meal?' She was quite striking in a perverse way. She wore a chartreuse-green dress that did its best to contain her ample girth, and enough rouge to do justice to the colouring of a butcher's sausage.

'No thanks, I'll be fine,' I said and the apparition disappeared back into the recess like a conger eel that had missed the prey.

I climbed the creaking stairs to Room 8 and found myself in another traditional setting – the bed had the obligatory sag in the middle and was covered in a frayed pink candlewick bedspread. I closed the door and felt a draught around my ankles. There was a gap at the bottom you could limbo under. Sitting on the edge of the bed I had a cigarette, then ran some hot water into the sink and freshened myself up.

After that I slept for a while then used the room facilities to make a coffee while channel hopping the television. Nothing interested me enough to watch it so I turned the volume low and searched for something to read. I discounted the Bible left by the Gideons and settled for a week old copy of the local evening paper I'd found under the bed. At nine I rang the Chinaman from the payphone downstairs. 'Let's rock n' roll,' I said.

Chapter 3

We got a taxi to the lower section of the Royal Mile with its medieval high-rise tenements. I paid the fare and asked for a receipt. The sky had cleared; hoarfrost sparkled from the pavement. We headed down a dark, steeply inclined cobbled street, cursing as we tried to keep our footing on the black ice.

'Choice location,' I said, surveying the decayed buildings on either side.

'Old storage vaults mainly,' said the Chinaman.

A few yards ahead a sharp beam of purple light flared from a doorway for a second or so. We stopped when we reached it.

'This is it,' said the Chinaman. He took off his suede gloves and undid his sheepskin coat.

I noticed there wasn't a name above the door advertising the establishment. We squeezed into a dim, all black entrance chamber the size of a compact lift with no apparent continuation. I presumed it had been deliberately designed like this to maximise the security. The only other occupant was a rotund bald bastard with no eyebrows, wearing a rubber jacket. On my left a curly-headed woman who resembled Harpo Marx, looked up at us from behind a two-foot square hole in the wall with sliding glass panels.

'Members only,' declared the doorman. He crossed his arms to emphasise his point.

'A friend recommended this place.' I said in a pleasant tone but the impasse remained.

The Chinaman brought out his cigarette case, opened it and proffered it towards the bouncer. The guy gave it a momentary glance and reached forward. To my surprise he swiftly extracted a twenty pound note and pocketed it. The Chinaman winked and snapped the case shut.

The doorman clenched his fist by his side. I prepared for a swift exit but he rapped on the wall and a door opened behind him. We were immersed in the purple light of the righteous. Just as we were about to step forward he jerked his head towards the woman. 'Pay the lady.'

The Chinaman indicated it was my shout. She mouthed 'Ten pounds' above the racket from within the club. I slid the note across. The doorman stood aside to let us through. Inside there were another couple of bouncers in dickey bow ties and evening suits. They glanced up for a second and then the door closed behind us.

'You owe me a drink,' said the Chinaman. We made our way round a pair of life-size golden statues of males in classical poses. They were nude and minus their fig leaves. I noted the stale smell of amyl nitrate and marijuana mingled with aftershave and sweat. Kylie Minogue belted out, '*I could be so lucky... lucky, lucky, lucky,*' from the dance area. I surveyed the crowd. Pretty boys abounded, along with short-haired dykes, but there were also punters who thought they were someone – shaven headed twats, pricks with Buddy Holly glasses, and leopard skin on cats that were for real.

I pulled out a tenner to wave at the bar staff. We were served instantly and I made a mental note to come here more often. I also noticed a glass behind the bar filled with what looked like spliffs.

'Whisky?' I asked the Chinaman. He nodded and scanned the darker recesses.

I thanked the barman as he placed the drinks on the counter. I asked him about the *special* cigarettes. 'Strictly for the sad, a pound each if you're interested.'

'Maybe later.' I passed a glass to the Chinaman. 'Any sign of our friend?'

'Don't see him.'

We found a vacant table in the chill-out area and waited. The Chinaman wanted to chat about old times but I was more interested in the present. I offered him a cigarette.

'How did you know where to photograph them?' I asked, catching a lustful look from a young guy standing at the bar. He wore a translucent black shirt that revealed his pierced nipples.

'Followed them from Jim Cowan's flat on Easter Road to here – simple as that.'

'When?'

'Friday.'

'Ever see Tony in here before?'

'What makes you think I frequent this joint?'

I peered into the gloom and clocked a couple of queens waving mistletoe towards the Chinaman. 'It's got your name written all over it Reuben.

'Okay, I pop in now and then – what's with the interrogation?'

'Just curious,' I said, unzipping my jacket.

'Look, I occasionally drift in here to see if I can spot anyone in the public eye who claims they're leading a saintly life... you know, politicians, Church of Scotland ministers – and listen out for any rumours.'

'Gossip that ruins people's lives more like.'

'It's what I do – once a newspaper hack, always a newspaper hack. It's an honourable profession I'll have you know. Anyway, since when have you become all moral? I wouldn't count what you do as being at the upper end of the food chain.'

'Okay,' I said, 'keep your corset on.' I flicked the ash from my cig into the aluminium ashtray on the table. 'What about the Bumble's brother? Ever see him in here?' Before he got a chance to answer I felt the presence of someone standing a bit too close for comfort. It was the pierced youth who had been staring at me.

'Like a dance?' He smiled and ran his fingers through his bleached quiff. The Pet Shop Boys thumped out '*You were Always on my Mind.*'

'Prefer the version by Elvis,' I said.

The Chinaman gave me a nudge and nodded in the direction of a table up the far end of the club on the other side of the dance floor. 'It's the Russian.'

I ignored the pass from my admirer and peered into the haze. A silver beam from a strobe lamp engulfed them.

The Russian seemed at ease, completely unaware of our presence. I reached into my pocket, brought out a twenty pound note, looked up at the youth and said, 'Keep my seat warm and my friend company – he'll buy the drinks.'

The lad didn't need a second invitation. He sat himself down uncomfortably close to the Chinaman on the scarlet velour bench seat.

'Thanks man! I'm Billy by the way.'

'Hey!' protested the Chinaman.

'Won't be long.' I said knowing I'd anchored him.

I figured the direct approach was the best tactic. I wove past several merry revellers who were in the festive spirit and adorned in silver tinsel and red Santa hats. One of them, a middle aged bloke, had blue Christmas baubles festooned to his nether regions – you could say he had balls.

The Russian's female companion kissed him hard on the lips as they sat at a table. I watched for a few seconds as her right hand moved down to his crotch. I guess he was getting an early Christmas present. The Russian's body twitched several times and he tightened his grip on her shoulder.

'Are you supposed to do that in here?' I said loudly. 'This is a gay club.'

He broke away from his *amour* and adjusted his attire. Then he located the nuisance who had interrupted his pleasure. Menace and hate swept his face as he clocked me.

His love interest looked up and said, 'You're allowed to do anything, sweetie. Everyone's allowed in... poofs, dykes, bis, even the odd straight... providing they're not expecting a peep show.' She tossed her shoulder length ash blonde hair like a defiant pony and I noticed her Adam's apple bobbing up and down. 'So what's your choice?'

'Psychopaths. Mind if I...?'

'Be my guest, honey.' She patted an empty chair on the other side of her.

'I need to speak to your man alone,' I said. 'Nothing personal.'

She kissed the Russian on the cheek and walked her fingers over the table to indicate she was taking a hike. 'Don't steal him away,' she said as she moved past me, her hand lightly brushing my thigh.

'He's not my type,' I said.

'Be gentle with him,' she cooed, and blew a kiss as she disappeared onto the dance floor.

I sat next to the Russian. 'You're not really that surprised to see me, are you?'

He shrugged. 'Maybe, maybe not – you are lucky man. I was going to kill you, break your stupid head.'

The cheaper the crook, the gaudier the patter as Sam Spade would say.

His eyes narrowed. 'What you want?'

'Justice and some information,' I said. 'Something your country knows little about... but for the moment, this.' I produced my wallet and eased out the embroidered Nazi eagle. I held it between two fingers for a moment, then allowed it to fall. It fluttered down in front of him. He took a slug of clear liquid from the shot glass beside him and fingered the cloth badge. His mind was contemplating something and it wasn't the price of caviar.

'You Fascist? Eh.'

'It comes with age. Tell Kev I want to talk, but not in Edinburgh, I'll meet him in Glasgow. Keep the badge.'

I didn't wait for a response and left him sitting there.

The Chinaman was still suffering the indignity of having company forced upon him. He rolled his eyes as he saw me approach. Billy, my new admirer, lifted a full pint glass of Stella and said, 'You're a lovely man.'

I smiled and perched on the seat next to them. The Chinaman forced a grin.

'What's your plans?' he said.

'None, except to watch our Russian friend's reaction.' I sat back.

'Watch what you're doing with that bastard!' Billy slurred. 'He's a bad, bad, bad man.' Before I could make any reply he leaned across and kissed me hard on the lips. I couldn't believe what he had just done and could only stare at him. No wonder women complain about stubble, I thought, rubbing my chin.

The Chinaman winked at us and laughed. 'It's only a question of aesthetics, nothing to be ashamed of.' He slugged back his whisky. He had a point, but right now I didn't feel like debating my sexuality.

'What's a kiss between friends?' said Billy. 'Besides we're in a gay club... who gives a hoot.' He stood up, a broad expression of mirth on his face. 'Want another drink?'

I looked past him and noticed that the seats previously occupied by the Russian and his trannie were empty. There was no point rushing out the door after them but I decided to go anyway.

'I'm off,' I said standing up.'

'Give us a hug then,' said Billy. He wrapped his arms around me and planted a kiss on my cheek.

Hell, there was no point in overreacting – when in Rome, I thought, and besides I might have to come back to the Pink Angel. I peeled him off, muttered a *Take care*, and glanced at the Chinaman. 'You coming?'

He shook his head. 'I'll stay for another drink. You'd be amazed at who you see in here...' he flourished his hand, 'and people are always grateful for information.'

'Send the bill to the Bumble,' I said.

I made my departure.

Jack Frost had now painted the town white and stars glittered in the heavens. I paused outside the entrance for a moment to light a fresh cigarette. Some leatherclad guys a few feet away were standing talking. A car made its way slowly down the cobbles and stopped beside them. A window lowered. 'Fucking faggots!' yelled one of the occupants. The car fishtailed on the icy surface as it roared off and the back seat passenger gave me the finger as they passed. I struck my Zippo, inhaled and watched the glow from the red taillights disappear.

I strolled up the street back towards the Royal Mile. A few snowflakes fell. I found a phone box and dialled the Bumble's mobile. It rang out and then went on to a message service. He must still be telling the truth, the whole truth and nothing but the truth to the cops about Tony. I flicked my cigarette into the night air, hailed a taxi and was gone.

Chapter 4

Come morning, I made a coffee in my room, had a smoke and called the Bumble.

'Christ,' he said 'the cops held us till almost midnight – any news your end?'

'Some,' I replied. 'See you at your office for eleven.' I declined breakfast from the elderly couple who ran the B&B and went to catch the best thing about Edinburgh – the Glasgow train.

An hour or so later, I strolled down from Queen Street Station through George Square with its statues to the great and the good. Someone had decorated the noble lions of the war memorial with purple tinsel. Multi-coloured festive lighting added brightness against the grey canopy of the sky.

The Duke of Wellington eyed me with suspicion from his plinth in Exchange Square, or maybe it was the humiliation of having a traffic cone stuck on his head that was pissing him off. Either way, I kept going.

A pang of hunger persuaded me to join the queue of punters at the Pantry Kitchen coffee shop on the corner of Argyle Street. I ordered a bacon roll and studied the chrome display units full of chocolate-and-cream bliss. It was a Faustian challenge to anybody on a diet. You could see the pineapple cakes, meringues and profiteroles urging you to devour them. It was almost sexual. This was a place where you could indulge yourself in cholesterol cunnilingus. I ordered a couple of chocolate doughnuts on the side and sat by the window contemplating my meeting with the Bumble.

An old geezer next to me in a tweed bunnet and raincoat prattled on about football. 'Good result the other night for the squad,' he said. 'Would'nae mind being there to see the lads in action for the next game.'

'Aye, good result.' I wolfed my bacon roll.

'Use your ashtray, son?'

'Help yourself.'

He seemed hell-bent on discussing Scotland's chances of winning the competition – which were nil – so I saved my breath and simply nodded at the right moments. He rattled on, hoping Scotland was on the glory trail.

I polished off the doughnuts and washed down my indulgence with coffee. Feeling marginally better, I lit a cigarette, zipped my jacket and strolled towards the Bumble's office ambling along the middle of the pedestrian precincts to avoid the zealots seeking seasonal cash for charity.

A deep rumble from the bridge above announced the arrival of another train into Central. I glanced at the numerous pigeons huddled under the blackened cast-iron girders and wondered if Stumpy ever did get his end away.

A short stroll later I was on Jamaica Street. The old red sandstone office blocks had once been the heart of the second city of the Empire. A lot of windows now displayed hardboard curtains that wouldn't have looked out of place in some war-torn country that had been ethnically cleansed. It wasn't an area to hang about in after dark. Several women on the game had been found dead not far from here, dumped like garbage down the Broomielaw beside the Clyde.

I glanced at a dull brass name plate attached to the wall:

D. A. Cowan Investigations
2nd Floor.

A lassie appeared out of the darkened entrance of the close – she must have been about early twenties – long dark hair with a typical Glasgow-Irish look, except any Celtic sparkle had long gone. Her eyes were dead and sunken, her soul long vanished. 'You wanting some business?' she said not looking at me directly.

'No, ta... not this morning, thanks,' I said, as though she was selling brushes on the doorstep. Well, in a sense I suppose she was. I offered her a cigarette and a light which she accepted without acknowledgement and went back to scanning the street for custom.

The second floor landing had little to recommend it beyond the smell of pish, dampness and vermin. The stair light must have been about the dimmest available in Glasgow and did nothing to reassure people there weren't all sorts of creepy crawlies waiting for them – two legged as well as four.

An elderly biddy passed me clutching the side of her face, a brown woollen tea cosy hat pulled firmly over her white locks. I gave her a *How do?* and she mumbled something in return and kept going. The Bumble's office, was next to Mr Klein, a practicing tooth puller, who had been here close on thirty years. He once had a lucrative business in the west end but got struck off for his addiction to the Novocain and being too liberal with the prescription pad. Most of his clients were now down at heel punters in need of denture repairs and a bit of sympathy.

I hoofed it along the landing to a door with the Bumble's name painted on a frosted glass panel in gold lettering outlined in black. I rapped the glass. A few seconds later a figure appeared, a key turned, and the door opened a couple of inches, restrained by a chain. The Bumble's nose poked out. 'How's it hanging?' I said.

'Och it's yerself. Come in.' The chain links rattled against the door frame as the Bumble slid the bolt back. The inner sanctum hadn't changed since I last saw it. There was still a saucer overflowing with cigarette butts sitting on the large oak desk. A bare bulb glowed from the ceiling, while an ancient two bar electric chrome fire supplied the heating. The wallpaper had once been magnolia, but was now well kippered from nicotine. The tan linoleum displayed assorted stains. On the wall hung a solitary calendar showing a picture of Christ preaching to the faithful, beneath which somebody had written in large black letters 'Employee of the Month'.

'I had a spiritual moment with the one your brother had on his wall.'

'Eh?' said the Bumble glancing up.

'The calendar.'

'Got it from an old Auntie,' said the Bumble, 'sends one out every year to all the members of the family. She hopes to save our souls.'

'An uphill struggle that one,' I said and drew back one of the ancient padded leather seats and sat down. I held my palms open to the heat from the fire and rubbed them together. 'A wee job you said, a day out in Edinburgh.'

'I know, I know,' said the Bumble. 'Honest to God I didn't think things would end up the way they did.' He clasped his hands together as though he was about to pray. 'Things have become a touch delicate.'

I pulled out a fresh packet of Marlboros from my jacket, peeled off the cellophane, scrunched the silver foil covering, and dropped it into an overflowing metal bin. 'A touch delicate? That's what you say in polite company when you tell folks about your haemorrhoids operation. What did you tell the cops?'

'Nothing. Just said I was doing the seasonal family bit by dropping in on my brother and nephew.'

'Did they believe you?'

He nodded. 'Eventually. They were all over me like a bad rash.'

'Why didn't you just phone your brother about Tony?' I said. 'Why did you need me to go over there?'

'Haven't spoken in years. We don't exactly get on. His *coming out* was the death of my mother...'

'Your mother was eighty four when she died, smoked and cursed like the proverbial trooper and wasn't averse to hard liquor.'

The Bumble shrugged, 'It was still a shock to her. You know how people of her generation took things. By the way, some bastard had obviously searched the place and the cops assumed I had done it.' He eyed me with suspicion.

'Must have been Kev Barr and the Russian when I was out cold.' I teased forward a cig from the packet and offered him one. 'I presume his mother now knows?'

His chins rippled as he gave another nod.

'How is she?'

'How the fuck do you think?'

He picked up a green plastic lighter, struck the mechanism a few times and succeeded in making fire. I used my Zippo.

'Look,' I said, 'I know it was personal between you and Tony but where does Kev Barr fit into this? It would have to be over drugs or tarts if he's involved, and since Bolivian marching powder doesn't seem to interest you, that would only leave pussy.'

'It's nae about tarts! Or drugs.'

I gave him a look. 'Got any coffee?'

'On the trolley by the window, make me one an' all.'

Opening a jar of cheap instant I put a teaspoon's worth of granules into a couple of heavily stained mugs. One had the star sign Capricorn – that was the Bumble, half man, half goat, licensed to shit in the street.

While waiting for the kettle to boil I looked out the window and watched the people below scurrying along going about their business. The kettle clicked off amid a cloud of steam. 'And there's now the problem of your missing brother,' I said, filling up the mugs.

The Bumble glowered in my direction. 'Tell me something I don't know.'

I went to put sugar in from an open bag and noticed small brown lumps that weren't the residue of coffee from a damp spoon. Mice, I thought. Contrary to belief, they have a sweet tooth. I sniffed the milk carton before topping up the coffee.

Placing a mug beside the Bumble I said, 'And the law, do they know your brother has probably been kidnapped?'

'What do you think Sherlock?'

I took a sip. 'Look,' I said, 'you asked me to work for you. I can take a walk.'

'C'mon, sit down – I suppose I owe you an apology, I didn't expect this to happen. It was meant to be a simple job.'

I stretched over towards the saucer that passed for an ashtray and tapped the arched column of ash from my cig.

The Bumble winced as he tasted the unsweetened coffee. 'Did ye no put sugar in? Christ!'

He went over and ladled several spoonsworth into the mug. I said, 'I wouldn't drink that Davie, mice have crapped in the sugar.'

'Has'nae done me any harm.' He sat himself back down.

'When I bumped into Kev in Edinburgh he said Tony'd tried to play smart, just like you.' I lifted my eyebrows. 'Wonder what he meant by that.'

The Bumble's porcine eyes narrowed. 'Okay, you might as well get the full score sooner rather than later – I guess you earned it.'

'You're all heart.'

He leaned down and pulled a drawer open lifting out a bottle of Glen Livet whisky. 'This is strictly for staff.'

'I'm honoured,' I said and blew a long stream of smoke towards a damp patch on the ceiling.

The Bumble poured generous measures into the coffees.

'A few weeks ago,' he said, taking a sip, 'I was asked to try and find any living relatives of an old dear who died...'

'So?' I said lifting my newly fortified beverage.

'So the person who asked me to enquire was Wilde.'

'Wilde?'

'Aye, Detective Chief Inspector Wilde. Mind of him?'

I nodded. I hadn't seen the guy since he was a Detective Sergeant out at Paisley. Always had an angle on something, just like the Bumble.

41

'Why? He could have done that through routine enquiries.'

'He didn't want any officialdom brought in. The old dear had been married to Peter Van Luben. You remember, years ago he held the only franchise in Scotland for certain German cars. They had a fancy showroom out Kelvinside.'

'Vaguely,' I said.

'Well,' said the Bumble easing back into his chair, 'there were rumours even when Van Luben was alive that the car franchise was a pay off for favours done, that he was in fact a Nazi.'

'A Nazi? Have you been at the funny fags?'

'No, look, you see, Van Luben claimed to be a Dutchman who came here during the war, a refugee from the Germans... but for someone who loathed the krauts he done alright out of flogging their cars. Anyway *he* died a year back and his widow a few weeks ago.'

I took a long slow draw on my cigarette. 'So where does Wilde fit into the picture?'

'Mrs Van Luben was found with a head injury and naturally the CID were asked in. It turned out to have been an accident, but by that time Wilde had turned the place over. He knew the rumours as well...'

'And decided to see if there was any Nazi loot,' I said.

'There wasn't,' said the Bumble, 'just a box full of old documents which Wilde gave to me for investigation purposes.'

'Why give you the documents?'

'Think about it – he couldn't exactly run things through proper channels... not if there was serious money hidden away.'

'And you of course would investigate for a slice of the pie.'

He shrugged. 'Naturally, like those ambulance chasing shyster lawyers – no win, no fee. It was my time and luck if anything came along.'

'And Wilde was happy about this?'

'I scratched his back many a time... and I know where the skeletons are buried. You forget Wilde and I started out together in the force. Both CID, both fellow members of the brotherhood.'

'I thought you're not meant to tell anybody?'

'Yeah, yeah.' The Bumble swallowed the remains of his refreshment.

As I said, like attracts like. 'Anyway, Wilde, he trusts you to confide in him if you find the lost treasures of the Third Reich here in sunny Glasgow? Want to know what I think? You've both been watching too many documentaries – you're both barking at the moon.'

The unmistakable high-pitched whine of a drill echoed from the dentist's office next door.

'That reminds me,' said the Bumble pushing his upper teeth forward with the tip of his tongue, 'I must get these falsers back to Mr Klein.'

I shuddered and took another sip of coffee. 'How did Tony fit into all this?'

'He was round at my flat one night when I'd a jar too many and crashed out. The bastard must have gone through the place and found some of the documents Wilde gave me from Van Luben's house.'

'And that's it?' I looked at him closely. The drill shrieked again.

'Tony had a curious nature... he took the various bits and pieces to a militaria dealer along the town, for a valuation. This guy knows he was onto something and practically bites Tony's hand off to buy them. Tony declines, because he knew that if this guy was willing to pay for them like that, then they had to be worth something.'

'How did you know that Tony had visited this militaria guy?'

'Kev Barr is a keen collector of Third Reich tat... developed the interest in prison. He's also a regular customer at this guy's militaria shop, by all accounts.'

'You surprise me,' I said.

'Kev came hammering on my door.'

'Did you tell him anything?'

'Give us a break. Do think I'm totally stupid?'

'Well...' I said, 'on the photograph the Chinaman took in Edinburgh, Tony had Kev's Russian sidekick beside him... and they looked quite chummy to me.'

'Maybe Tony called him.'

'Possible,' I said.

'Maybe it was a deal that went wrong. Maybe Tony got greedy.'

'Why would Kev Barr come back?' I said, 'Tony had been dead for at least twenty-four hours judging by state of him.

'Forgotten something?'

'Like the documents?'

'Maybe,' said the Bumble.

'Doesn't add up. They would have ransacked the place there and then when they'd killed him. If they killed him.'

There was silence for a moment. The Bumble raised his index finger to tap ash from his cigarette and paused. 'You've got them, haven't you? The documents?'

'What about a finders fee?' I said and dug out my fags.

'Finders fee?'

'Yeah, if they're that valuable then a bonus should be due me.'

The Bumble pondered the request then remembered. 'Hell I gave you a wad in Edinburgh.'

I pointed to my head. 'That covered the trauma I received. You wouldn't have anything without me.'

'Okay,' said the Bumble, 'since it's Christmas.' He scooped out a hundred quid from his wallet.

'That all I'm worth?'

'What is this? A hustle or something?'

I blew a smoke ring at him, it hovered above his bald patch like a halo. 'Do I have to remind you,' I said, leaning forward, 'of what's happened in the last few days? Murder, assault and kidnapping – and I'm in the front line. You've given me a far-fetched tale about Nazis and then hand me a hundred quid – c'mon.'

'Okay, okay,' said the Bumble and doubled the offer.

I slung the green book on the desk and lit my cig.

'See,' said the Bumble reaching across, 'that's why I employ you – you're a resourceful man. Your time on the force was'nae wasted after all.' He poured more whisky into my mug. 'Cheers! Mind I expect a birthday present.'

'Birthday present?'

'You're still coming to my party tonight.'

'Party?'

'Christ, you've forgotten. It's my birthday.'

'No,' I said, 'I haven't. Just thought under the circumstances...'

'No point in sack-cloth and ashes.' He filed the whisky in the drawer beside him. 'Let's show the world it's business as usual.'

Chapter 5

The Bumble told me to take the rest of the afternoon off. He was generous that way. I scooped up the junk mail from behind my front door – Christmas cards, bills and flyers from the local takeaways and dropped them next to the kettle. Momentarily, I studied the selection on offer from Mings Cantonese restaurant and the exciting Christmas offer of a quality bottle of German wine and prawn crackers with every banquet meal.

I made some tea and several slices of toast with crunchy peanut butter and tried to relax in the worn and armchair by the gas fire. The chair had belonged to my grandmother – devotees of Freud would say I was seeking a bit of comfort. They'd be right. I worked my way through the mail, momentarily remembering acquaintances and the odd relative who wished me a 'Merry Christmas' or 'All the Best'.

Eventually, I lay down and slept for a few hours. When I woke, I freshened up and phoned Charlie McLeod. 'Going to the big party? Fine, any chance of a lift from Central Station to the Bumble's flat? What do you mean, what am I after?'

Hail bounced off the glass roof of Central like lead shot on plate armour as I strolled down the platform to the main concourse. I lit a cig and studied the usual assortment of punters that frequent stations after the sun goes down.

'Hi! Could I show you the work that we do?'

I half turned to see this Asian-looking girl with a small red mark on her forehead. She was holding a clipboard. I switched off as she launched into the sales drive. I took a deep draw on my cigarette and presumed she was some type of Hari Krishna. I thought of asking her whatever happened to their orange outfits – maybe they had sold them to the Loyalists in Ulster for the marching season – aye, *The Sari My Father Wore*. Perhaps she saw a tormented soul, eager to gain salvation by being relieved of his wealth, as she ended the sales pitch by assuring me she'd even take a cheque. I found a few coins and gave them to her. 'Sorry, it's all I've got.'

'I have only one thing to ask of you!' she declared. 'I would like you to call out Gouranga!'

She enlightened me that it meant 'Be happy!' Fat chance, I thought and dropped my cigarette to the ground, crushing it underheel. As I did so I caught the strained voice of an acned youth with a white baseball cap sitting on a bench: 'Ah'm fucking straight ah tell ye!'

Either he had been apprehended by his parole officer or the punter sitting next to him with a face like a well-skelped arse was on a hiding to nothing.

I shivered and zipped up my leather jacket. Out of the corner of my eye I saw a familiar figure that could cast a long shadow. It was Charlie McLeod. He was a big-built ex cop of the type the force used to like to recruit – simple mind and strong back. These days he was a precognition agent for solicitors on a freelance basis. In reality he took statements from neds and other low life in their hovels, before their court appearances. Occasionally, the Bumble would employ him for the odd job that didn't require tact. I watched him scratch his greying moustache while he looked up and down the station. Then he marched towards me like Joe Stalin on his way to a show trial for a bit of entertainment. 'Yer late.'

No 'How are you?' or 'How's the health.' But that was Charlie – no shades of grey, only black and white. He'd been like that since we'd met at police training college twenty years ago.

'The car's outside,' he said, 'c'mon.'

We left through the side entrance down the steps onto Union Street. Sleet pelted down like gobs of spit. Revellers huddled in doorways for cover but Charlie strolled as though it was a summer's day. About half way down the street we stopped beside his pride and joy – a 1970's Ford Capri, with a Vitamin C orange paint job complemented by a black vinyl roof. Charlie unlocked the driver's door, got in and leant across to unlock the passenger's side. It opened with a creak and I climbed in and closed the door.

The time-warped machine burst into life and a warm blast of air filtered through the vents. Charlie put the car into gear and we accelerated into the flow of the evening traffic. I sank back in my seat and took a look at the state of the interior with its collection of fish and chip papers.

'Still into a healthy lifestyle I see.'

'Gave up the fags. One thing at a time. Besides what are you worried about? Life's terminal anyhow.' He had a droll humour. 'If you're still cold there's a bottle in the glove compartment.'

I opened it and took out the half bottle of Grouse, unscrewed the cap and took a swig. It burned all the way down. I grimaced as I took another slug. Tartan tradition, can't live with it, can't live without it.

'Use yer fucking eyeballs ya eejit!' shouted Charlie, as a young guy in white trousers and a blue denim jacket jumped for the pavement. His trousers caught the tidal wave from the gutter, as we roared past. I turned and watched him gesturing and shouting in our direction and I didn't need a translator. I laughed, feeling more relaxed and reached into my pocket for a cigarette. Then I noticed the *No Smoking* sign stuck on the dashboard. Nothing like the converted.

'So did you get the Bumble a present then?' I said.

He looked across and raised his eyebrows which I took for *You must be joking.* 'Did you?'

I held up a carrier bag containing a bottle of whisky.

Charlie picked a toffee from a paper poke in the centre consul, unwrapped it, flicked the silver foil behind him and chewed. I turned on the radio and some inane techno music thumped out followed by a Glasgow DJ with an affected mid-Atlantic twang.

'Got anything better than that?' I said.

'See what you think of this.' Charlie pushed a cassette into the stereo.

For a minute I couldn't work out what it was and then it clicked. 'This *The Sash?*'

'Like it? It's the re-mix version from the Shankhill Boyz Band, got it at the Barras market last week. Different isn't it?'

Christ Almighty, what was traditional sectarianism coming to? I thought of the seventeenth century Protestant Irish supporters of King Billy who had originally marched to the fifes and drums of this song and pictured their puzzlement and horror at such treatment of a sacred anthem for their cause.

We headed past rows of shops and tenements along Great Western Road with the sleet getting heavier by the minute. 'I hear things got a bit hairy over in Edinburgh,' said Charlie.

'Yeah,' I said, 'that's one way of describing it.' I opened the glove compartment, took another slug of whisky and screwed the metal cap back on with a firmness that would keep the Genie secure.

'Could be worse,' said Charlie, 'You could be down the morgue with a tag on yer big toe lying next to Tony.'

'So you've heard?'

Charlie nodded. 'Kev must have got counselling while he was inside at the Bar-L. By rights you should be deid.'

'Thanks,' I said and hesitated about taking another measure of whisky.

'Well, ye helped put him in the big hoose.'

'I suppose. But there's something not right about it all.'

'Want my advice?' said Charlie as he slowed the Capri to a halt, 'stay clear. There's plenty other work out there, hell I could fix you up with a job like mine.'

'I'll think about it.'

'Well, don't think to long if you want to stay alive.'

We parked outside a familiar Victorian tenement on Dumbarton Road. I opened the car door to the final chorus from *The Sash*.

'By the way,' said Charlie, 'you can crash at our place tonight if you want, save you hiking back home to Langside.'

'Thanks, might just do that.'

Several flights of stairs later we paused on the top floor. We could hear music and muffled voices. I was breathless.

'You should give up the fags,' said Charlie, rapping his knuckles on a door.

Aye nothing like the converted.

The door opened and there stood the Bumble – still a fat bastard. He was pished. A red paper hat crowned his head while a half smoked cigarette hung from the corner of his mouth. 'Come away in!' he said as we stepped into his web. He gave me a bone-crushing handshake and a wink.

'Happy Birthday,' I said and handed him his present.

'Och you shouldn't have bothered. We'll have a wee word later eh? Pleasure first!' He strolled off down the hall examining the bottle of *Auld Jock* I'd got from my local corner shop. The proprietor had assured me that Taiwan made excellent whisky.

Charlie nudged me. 'C'mon lighten up, let's get a drink.'

I followed him past an assortment of punters into the kitchen. Charlie went straight to the fridge.

'Lager or Heavy?'

'Lager,' I said, accepting a can of Stella. I pulled the ring and took a sip. It tasted good. The dryness in my mouth eased and I took my cigarettes from my pocket. Charlie wandered off but I decided to stay where I was. I sat on a kitchen stool by the open window and took a deep draw, blowing the smoke out into the night air. The kitchen was quiet. A couple of women in party dresses talked about the office asshole and who he had tried it on with this week, while a few guys spouted the usual football tripe. I felt a tap on my shoulder and turned round to see a woman standing next to me.

'Hi stranger, long time no see.'

I could do nothing but look at her. She was as inviting as ever with that golden hair, pale skin and emerald green eyes. I used to call her my Celtic Princess, except it made her sound like a Clyde paddle steamer. It was Heather McCann the Bumble's much younger cousin.

'How're you doing?' I said, for the want of anything better.

'Not bad, and you?' She smiled a knowing smile, as if she knew something I wasn't privy to.

'Pretty good.' I took another draw on my cig then flicked it out into the night air. I watched it fall like a burned out star to the garden below. I took a swig from the can.

She offered me another cigarette, 'Still living out at Langside?'

'Yeah, still there. You should come over some time.'

'That an invite?'

'Maybe,' I said giving her a carnal look.

Heather smiled, her eyes sparkling. 'My partner wouldn't like it.'

'Didn't know you were involved. Is he here?'

There was a pause; I think it's called a pregnant pause.

'Yes, *she's* here. That's her over there.' She nodded in the direction of a woman with short dark hair and a scowl.

My jaw must have gone slack at the prospect of Heather having become a lesbian. I lit our cigarettes trying not to look too unfazed. 'So what are you up to?'

'Started a small cafe-cum-night club with Kyde,' she said, smiling over at her partner.

'Unusual name,' I said. 'What is it, Greek or something?'

'No,' said Heather, 'it's an anagram of dyke.'

'Original.'

'Drop in sometime,' she said with a hint that could promise more, 'our place is called the Minge Tout, just along Byres Road.'

'Very fitting.' I wondered what else had changed around here. Then I became aware of someone else standing beside me. It was Kyde. I looked her up and down and clocked the number of piercings she had, from her eyebrows to her tongue. She looked intent on doing the jealous lover routine.

'I'm Heather's parthner,' she lisped. The studs must've been mangling her tongue. She noticed me studying her piercings and decided to assess my shockability rating. 'I've got a pierthed clitorith as well,' she said.

'Give you a ring sometime then, doll,' I quipped.

Heather put an arm around Kyde and moved off with a 'Catch you later.'

I watched her getting interrogated, no doubt about me, judging by the filthy looks I was getting. Returning my gaze to the night outside I watched as snow now fell. I got up and went in search of the bog.

I studied my reflection in the mirror above the lavatory seat. There seemed to be more lines than this morning and more grey at the sides of my head. There was a loud knock on the door and a guy shouted, 'Hey! C'mon I'm bursting for a pish out here!' I flushed the toilet, gave the hands a quick rinse and opened the door to a man in a worse state than I was. 'Christ man, I'm fucking bursting!' With that the toilet door slammed behind him.

The hallway was still full of people. From the lounge Andy Williams sang *'Take my hand, take my whole world too'*. I spotted the Bumble speaking to a woman in her late thirties with heavy mascara and long black back-combed hair. She wore a sparkling silvery low cut evening dress and had several tattoos – one of the young Elvis on her upper arm and a red rose nestling on her right breast. I also wondered how she remained upright in her stilettos, which made her eye-level with the Bumble.

The Bumble insisted I join him. 'The very man!' he slurred, putting an arm around my shoulder so I could have the full appreciation of his halitosis and lack of deodorant. He paused and I thought he was going to kiss me. 'It's good of ye to come and see the Bumble on his birthday.'

I smiled. 'Aye.'

He took a slow sip from his glass then put a fresh cigarette between his lips and looked round asking if anyone had a light. Only an old guy with a tired face bothered to look at him, even then it was to shrug his shoulders and say he had given up smoking and that the Bumble should do likewise. For a moment the Bumble stared at the guy then said, 'You ma fucking faither? Nae bastard got a light? Nae bastard smoke these days?'

I fumbled in the pocket of my denim shirt and gave him a lighter with a picture of two topless bronzed girls on it. I had acquired it somewhere on a holiday.

'See, that's why I employ you, you always come up trumps!' He lit the cigarette and I told him to keep the lighter. He smiled so much at the gift, I thought that in a previous life he must have been one of the Indians who were happy to swap New York for a handful of glass beads. He studied the two beauties from all angles. His female companion was unimpressed, so he groped her bum. 'Yer still the best!' he said, as though she had just won the shag of the week award. He turned his attention back to me. 'So do you fancy another wee job?'

'So long as it doesn't involve a contest,' I said, 'with my head and a baseball bat. Do you want to talk somewhere else?' I glanced at his *amour*.

The Bumble took another sip of his whisky and said, 'Oh don't mind her. I've got no secrets from Priscilla.' His nose grew so much that it could feature in a porn movie by itself. I looked at Priscilla, who was yawning, and then at the Bumble.

'Look,' he said, 'come round to the office in the morning. Here! You have'nae a drink. Have a drop of this.' He found a tumbler on the hall table that already contained the dregs of piss-coloured wine. Pouring a large measure of the whisky I'd bought for him into it he handed it to me. The Bumble knocked back his own drink and grimaced. I did the same. Priscilla whispered into his ear, her dark eyes bored.

'Listen,' he said, flicking his cigarette ash onto the carpet. 'I'll have more time to talk to you tomorrow. Back to the pleasures of the flesh.' He groped Priscilla's behind again. 'Oh,' he added, 'and thanks for coming.'

For some reason I felt like the goat that had been invited to the grand tiger hunt. I wandered back up the hall and into the lounge. Charlie was sitting on the settee engrossed in conversation with the Bumble's sister Linda who was suitably attired in a low cut black velvet dress. Her ginger locks had been permed into the big hair look while her cleavage would have put Pamela Anderson to shame.

'Sorry about Tony,' I said.

She looked up. 'Thanks,' she said and slugged back the clear contents of her glass without any register of emotion. She leaned forward to pick up a sausage roll from a plate on the table in front of her ensuring I had an ample view of her bosom. 'Maybe we can talk sometime?'

'Yeah,' I said, 'give us a call.'

She sat back, looked directly at me and placed her lips around the end of the pastry. I watched her masticate.

Linda dusted off a few flakes of pastry from her chest and dabbed her ruby red lips with a piece of white kitchen paper. I glanced at the perfect imprint of her lips on the makeshift napkin. She languorously reached forward for her cigarettes on the table. 'So tasty don't you think?'

I nodded. She had always reminded me of a cat, a marmalade cat.

'Catch you later,' I said and went in search of another drink. There wasn't a hint of grief about her over Tony but there again, loss can do strange things to people. Maybe she was putting a brave face on.

I hung about for a while chatting to various folk that I vaguely knew and by eleven I'd had enough. My jacket had been thrown into what I presumed was a bedroom. I half-opened the door of the darkened room and was fumbling for the light switch when I heard low moans and a persuasive male voice saying, 'Oh go on'. I coughed. 'Hey!' he said. 'Can we no have some privacy in here?'

Fuck it I thought, I want my jacket and I also want out of here. So I went ahead and switched on the light.

'Hey! What the fuck! You fucking pervert! Switch the fucking light out and fuck off!'

I spotted my jacket wedged under a young woman. She was attempting to cover herself up but only succeeded in revealing her buttocks. She had some sort of tattoo on her left cheek that resembled a squashed spider. Maybe that's what it was. I whipped my jacket casually from under her.

'Fuck off mister,' said the lassie, 'or I'll get ma uncle to chuck you out!'

'Oh, and who might that be?'

'The Bumble.'

I laughed.

'Aye! He'll sort you out!'

I laughed even more when I saw the scrawny pasty-faced teenager propping his frame up on pipe-cleaner legs, while covering his privates with his hands. I switched the light off. 'Sorted by the Bumble, that's a good one.'

'Dirty bastard!' he shouted after me as I closed the door.

Pushing past people who had become inquisitive at the stooshie, I opened the main door and left. Making my way down the stairs I looked at the old brass name plates, some of which were polished until the names had been worn down. A bit like life itself. I reached the bottom of the stairs and lit another cigarette. As I strolled out into the cold night air, I found myself whistling the traditional version of *The Sash*.

Chapter 6

I pulled back the curtains the next morning to a grey overcast day. After a wash and a bowl of muesli that would have passed for cat litter I caught the underground, affectionately known as the Clockwork Orange, on account of the system running on a loop, and the colour of the carriages. I got off in the city centre at St Enoch's Station, bought a couple of packets of cigarettes and strolled round to Jamaica Street.

The Bumble was at his desk.

'Anybody else die or been abducted since yesterday?' I said, heading for the kettle.

He sighed, sat back down and lifted a Marks and Spencer carrier bag onto the desk. Reaching into it he brought out an old brown teddy bear with amber eyes. It had a hangman's noose around his neck. There was silence for a moment. 'Didn't know Sooty was a Mason,' I said.

'It arrived by courier this morning,' said the Bumble. 'It belongs to my brother, Jim. I recognise it from when we were kids. There was a phone call from Kev Barr saying he had him.'

'So,' I said, 'I presume he's being held here in Glasgow?'

The Bumble nodded.

I poured boiling water into a couple of mugs and spooned in coffee. 'Here, I bought some sweeteners – want some?

'Aye, go on.'

Opening the window I lifted the carton of milk on the sill and checked to see if the birds had been at it. It seemed safe enough to drink.

'So,' I said, 'what's the price for not hanging your brother?' I handed a mug to the Bumble.

'The documents.'

'Okay, what do they want to do? Meet and exchange?'

'You been watching the Ipcress File again? This is'nae the Cold War with the KGB, we're not about to meet in an underground carpark – this is Kev Barr we're dealing with.'

'How long have we got?'

'By six tonight,' said the Bumble.

He brought out the old black and white photograph and the green passport sized book and laid them on the desk.

'Did you find out anything more about them,' I said and threw a cig towards him?'

He picked up the photograph. 'The woman in the photograph is Mrs Van Luben.'

'I don't suppose you've got a name for the guy beside her?'

'No.'

'Okay what's so special about the book that people are willing to kill and kidnap for?'

'This,' said the Bumble picking it up, 'is a pass for a Swiss bank account.' He leaned across the desk, 'You know the story about Rudolf Hess flying to Scotland?'

'A wee bit,' I said.

'Came down south of the city,' said the Bumble, 'out at Eaglesham, in May 1941 to be precise. He allegedly came here on some sort of peace mission – supposedly to see the Duke of Hamilton – quite why, nobody knew, including the Duke.'

'But everybody thought he was a numptyheid, including the Nazis,' I said. 'Christ, I read somewhere that Adolf went into a rage when he heard, and chewed the carpet.'

'Hess was'nae such a nutter as you think, he was legging it to the United States,' said the Bumble.

'To the States? How could he do that?' I said.

The Bumble smiled. 'Easier than you think. You see the United States was still neutral in May 1941 and there were plenty of ships plying back and forth from the Clyde to America.'

'What? He flew here, bailed out and expected to buy a one way ticket to the US?' I began to think the Bumble had lost the plot.

'It went wrong,' said the Bumble with authority.

The phone rang, he picked it up and in his best-polished accent said, 'Cowan Investigations how may I help?' he listened for a moment. 'Give me your details... this evening, fine.' He scribbled an address on a note pad and cradled the receiver. 'A client, thinks his wife is up to no good with a member of staff. Anyway, where was I? Aye, you see from what I gathered from various histories I've researched, Hess was being tracked on radar and had fighters on his tail, which forced him off course. He was within minutes of being shot down and possibly killed, so he had to bail out in the wrong place.'

'But I still don't get it.'

The Bumble slid back a drawer in the desk beside him and brought out a couple of books and placed them on the table. They both pertained to Hess. He opened one at a marked spot.

The Bumble pointed to a photograph, which showed Hess and a young girl who looked a lot like Mrs Van Luben.

The Bumble gave a smug smile and said,' Mrs Van Luben arrived here in 1940, according to records, as a refugee.

I studied the photograph in the book. 'Okay, it looks like her... so, how does America fit into all this?'

'In the documents that Wilde gave me there was also an identity card with a photo of a guy who looked a lot like Rudolf Hess. The card was in the name of Anton de Nervalle, a supposed refugee from Belgium.'

'Let me guess,' I said, 'Van Luben was his man in Glasgow.'

'Exactly!' The Bumble went into the desk drawer again and brought out some faded buff cards with official stamps on them and placed them on the table. 'Good job Tony didn't take everything, eh?'

I picked one of them up and studied it. It was a boarding pass for a ship called the SS Dunglass dated May 15th 1941 and was made out in the name of Anton de Nervalle.

'But how did you know that the ship was sailing to the United States?' I asked.

'I done a bit of research on that as well, through the Imperial War Museum and they were able to tell me the routes of the ship for 1941. She was heading to New York on the night of the 15th May.' The Bumble smiled even more. He was the cat that had discovered cream in his bowl. 'I told you I was onto something big, didn't I? Can't just hand all this over to that bastard Kev Barr though.'

'Why not? I'm not being cynical Davie, or knocking your research but it's just a bunch of old papers. There's nothing to say where X marks the spot, is there? The whole thing could be one big hoax.' I yawned. 'So what's next? Or is that it?'

From the inside of his jacket pocket he brought out a white envelope and handed it to me.

'Go on open it and have a read.'

There were two letters inside, one fresh, the other on faded paper. The older letter was written in German while the more recent was in English.

'It's a translation,' said the Bumble picking up my packet of Marlboros, 'of an authorisation letter to make a withdrawal from a Swiss bank not far from the German border. Hess took off from an airfield in the same region.'

When I had finished reading, I gave out a low whistle. 'Nice if it's true.'

'Course it's fucking true! Hess was'nae going to sit out the rest of his days on social security, was he?'

Once again the Bumble went into his jacket pocket, brought out another envelope and carefully took out a faded slip of white paper and handed it to me. At the top there was an embossed crest and some writing, again in German; it had also been officially stamped and signed.

It's a withdrawal receipt,' he said.

I looked at it and the date of the stamp – April 30th, 1941, a few days before Hess flew here.

'So?' I said, 'All it proves is that someone made a withdrawal. The loot, if there is any, could be anywhere from the bottom of a loch to South America.'

The Bumble took a deep draw and sighed as he blew the smoke out. 'You don't get it, do you? It was Hess that took the gold and flew here with it!' He thumped the table making the mugs clink.

'It's still fantasy fucking island Davie, it's all circumstantial, you of all people should know that.'

He bent down and lifted a Tesco supermarket bag towards me and said, 'Go on have a look at what's inside this.'

I went to grab it and noticed how heavy it was. I sat it on my lap and looked inside at something wrapped in newspaper. I peeled the paper back to reveal a bar about six inches long – it shone with lustre. Christ! It was a fucking gold ingot. I glanced at the Bumble. 'This real?' I said.

'Course it's fucking real ya bampot! Do you think I'd fall for it if it was'nae? Look underneath it.'

I turned it over and saw it carried a serial number along with a Nazi eagle.

'Give it back here! Believe me it's fucking real, one hundred percent pure gold.'

'So where's the rest?'

'That's the problem,' he said. 'I don't know.'

'What do you mean? You don't know? Where did this one come from?'

The Bumble tapped the side of his nose. 'Searched the Van Luben house myself, knew that Wilde and his woodentops wouldn't do a thorough job.

'And that was it? One solitary gold bar. Nothing else?'

The Bumble shook his head. 'But think about it, there has to be more, I just know Hess brought a crateful with him, I just fucking know.'

I stroked my stubble and pondered matters.

'Right now though,' said the Bumble, 'we've got to sort out that bastard Kev Barr and that brother of mine. Listen, I've been thinking... we could give Kev this gold bar in exchange for Jim.'

I was taken aback by his suggestion. 'Are you sure?'

'It's the only way, cos if we give Kev the documents then our chances of getting them back will be slim and Swiss banks won't accept photocopies.'

'Aye, I suppose you're right,' I said.

'I know I've got a bit of a nerve to ask,' said the Bumble, 'but would you do the necessary? Take the gold and try and get Jim back? Kev might go for a bird in the hand. I wouldn't blame you if you refused point blank... but I'll more than make it worth your while. Look, I've more work than you can shake a stick at and I'd been thinking of making you a partner – who better than someone I trust?' He reached into his jacket that was draped over the back of the chair and produced a roll of banknotes. 'Another five hundred – what do you say?'

Inside my head someone screamed at me to turn it down. I swirled coffee round my gums, swallowed and said, 'Okay, I'll go and speak to Kev – but it's an equal partnership or nothing.'

The Bumble nodded eagerly. 'Of course, of course. I wouldn't forgive myself if Jim ended up like Tony. Take the gold and see if you can trade it for him – his life is worth that much if not more.' He added a touch more whisky to the mugs, raised his in salute and said, 'Partner.'

We clinked the cups and I heard myself saying, 'I'll get him back for you.' I rubbed my head where I'd clobbered it on the table. Maybe the blow was affecting my judgement. 'What's the address for the meet?'

'Kev Barr's pub. It's out the east end of the city.'

'I know it,' I said.

'Get Jim and convince Kev that's all I have.' He placed the supermarket bag on the desk with a solid *clunk*.

I glanced at it, shoved the money into my top pocket and zipped it closed. 'Need to pay a visit. Back in a minute.'

While I relieved myself, I wondered why I was really going to do this deed. Nothing occurred to me so I shrugged, gave the matter in hand a shake and thought that greed was a good a motive as any. I dropped my fag into the yellowish water, it hissed for a second then I pulled the chain and washed my hands.

'You might need this,' said the Bumble when I got back. He unwrapped an oiled cloth and took out a heavy vintage revolver. 'Give you an edge.'

I studied the hardware for a second. 'A Webley .45 – stops just about anything short of an elephant.'

'Belonged to my grandfather,' said the Bumble, 'Used it against the Huns on the Somme.'

'Haven't seen one in years.' I pushed a catch on the side and broke the gun open. Six brass cases smiled back from the chambers. I clicked it shut. 'I don't know about this, I could end up on a firearms charge.'

'You could also end up stripped naked and tortured with a rope around your neck.'

I hesitated for a second, wrapped the cloth round it and shoved it into the carrier bag. 'If things don't work out...'

'They will,' said the Bumble with a confident air. 'They will.'

Chapter 7

The Hole in The Wall was a traditional boozer that nestled into its backdrop of the east end of the City. It wasn't on the Glasgow Tourist Board guide for its originality. It wasn't on anyone's guide other than for good ole white trash. The taxi driver asked if I wanted him to wait after I told him my trip to the establishment was strictly business. 'No mate, you're alright – thanks.' I tipped him the price of a pint for his concern.

Pushing the re-enforced heavy wooden doors, I entered the gloominess of the hostelry. I was greeted by an electronic Phil Mitchell from *Eastenders*. 'Alright Bruv?' Yeah, well sorted Phil. It was a one-armed bandit that featured the voices of the characters from the well-known soap.

The place was comparatively empty. A couple of youths in Celtic scarves gave us a quick glance and a few old blokes sat round a table chewing the fat. Framed scenes from Celtic's glory days lined the walls and cigarette smoke hung in the air. A yellow-fringed banner with red lettering was strung from the gantry that stored the spirits, wishing the clientele *Merry Christmas*.

A large guy whose black leather jacket didn't quite meet over his beer gut leaned on the bar counter and sized me up.

His greasy wavy hair was slicked back Teddy boy fashion. Long sideburns stretched along his jaw. He rolled a wafer thin cigarette that wouldn't give more than two draws and a spit. I clocked the black and tan Rottweiler at his feet.

To the side of the bar sat a fat woman. Her hair was bleached blonde and tied back from her face, which only served to make her look harder. Tattoos covered her bare forearms. She ignored my intrusion. I noticed that she was reading a copy of True Crime – probably to see if anyone she knew featured.

The dog gave a deep growl. The guy smiled, struck a match and lit his roll up cigarette.

'I have a bit of business to talk about,' I said, 'with the boss that is.'

He sucked on his roll up and gestured towards an empty chair beside the fat woman. I sat down and brought out my packet of cigs. She ignored me, still engrossed in her publication.

The guy hauled the dog over and sat next to me.

'I'm a friend of the Bumble's,' I said lighting up.

He took another draw on his rollie and squashed it flat in the ashtray. 'Is that a recommendation?' he said. The Rottweiler growled some more under the table and then casually stretched out on the floor. Its eyes remained open, studying me as though he couldn't quite place where we had last met.

I flicked the ash off my cig onto the mutt.

The guy grinned and I noticed his stained teeth, the same colour as his fingers, mottled mustard and brown. I eyed up the two reptiles with shaved heads and no necks who appeared from nowhere and sat at the bar. They looked ready to carve me up if Tango didn't get there first.

'This one of those theme pubs?' I said inhaling. 'You know, like you get Irish ones except this one is for scum?' Again I flicked my ash onto Tango. 'I want to talk to Kev Barr, he owns this dump doesn't he?'

'He might do. Suppose he doesn't want to talk to you?'

'He will,' I said.

'Sure of yourself, aren't you?'

In the background the electronic Phil Mitchell still enquired after my health: 'Alright, Bruv?'

Yeah Phil, still doing okay – so far. I went back on the offensive.

'You don't think I'd be daft enough to walk in here without some backup?' I decided to cut to the chase and withdrew the gun from the carrier bag. Instantly one of the thugs at the bar produced a sawn off shotgun and levelled it at me. Punters made a hasty exit from the bar. A few seconds went by then a door slid back behind the counter and Kev Barr appeared. He stood there eyeing us up and down then laughed, loudly. Tango barked in approval of his hilarity, just like the last time we met.

'Well, well,' I said, 'look who's popped his head out of his hole.'

Kev said nothing. The hoodlum with the shotgun still had it levelled at me. I gazed at the guy sitting beside me and wiggled the gun about for effect. 'This is a Webley .45 service revolver to be precise. Old I know, still very effective though at blowing bastards like you into a squashed beef tomato... oh and it's loaded with hollow points, ever see what they can do? Special Forces still use them for getting up close and personal.'

Okay, that part I'd read somewhere in an Andy McNab novel. I cocked the trigger just to make sure they got the message. I moved the gun in the direction of the guy's stomach and glanced sideways at the woman who was still reading the magazine. Her lips moved as she read the words. 'Kev, does she ever pay attention to what goes on round here? Is she deaf or what?'

'Take a walk, Senga,' he said and the woman got up and disappeared towards the toilets.

'Ho! Mick,' he shouted to the guy across the table from me. 'Get out of that chair and bring over a couple of whiskies, mind not the cheap crap for the regulars, the good stuff. You like whisky don't you?'

I had no option but to nod. Mick scowled in my direction then got up and did as he was told.

Kev wandered over and sat down opposite me giving the gun the once over. I placed it on the table within easy reach. Two whiskies arrived. Kev lifted his glass. 'Cheers!'

I watched him and reached for the other glass with my left hand.

'Tommy, I think we can dispense with the hardware,' Kev said and the guy put the sawn-off shotgun back behind the counter. I left the big revolver where it was.

'You know,' said Kev, 'you must have cojones the size of coconuts.'

I felt my stomach churn over – nerves and too much whisky.

'By the way,' Kev went on, 'I enjoyed that little show we had in Edinburgh. And thanks for the wee gift of the Nazi eagle ye sent me. I've added it to my collection. Early Luftwaffe, quite rare, probably a German flyer that took part in the Spanish civil war. Franco, now there's a man ye could do business with.'

'While we're on the theme of international criminals,' I said, 'where's your pet Russian?' I threw the whisky down my throat in one.

'You've been watching too many John Wayne movies,' said Kev, eyeing my empty glass. 'You should sip a good malt slowly. The Russian? Oh he's down in the cellar entertaining the Bumble's brother. Loves his work does Trotsky.'

'Christ Almighty,' I muttered. 'Jim Cowan had better be unharmed, otherwise you'll get nothing of what I've got to offer. I want to see him now!' I lifted the carrier bag on to the table with a clunk.

Kev glanced at it with curiosity. 'Mick, go get him up here.' Kev and I sat eyeballing each other.

I heard the cellar trap door being lifted, then footsteps. I looked over to see Jim Cowan being led up by the Russian. Trotsky grinned as he shoved Jim in our direction.

Jim Cowan looked rough but he brightened up when he saw me.

'You okay Jim?'

He nodded.

'You see,' said Kev, 'he's unharmed. Now my friend, life has to be a game of give and take. Right now I'm going to take and you're going to give – comprende?' Kev held his hand out towards me.

'I don't have what you want.'

Kev's expression changed, his eyes narrowed and he became more like his old self from years ago. His top lip disappeared and his whole persona became mean. He gave a nod towards one of the hired hands to get the sawn-off back out.

Jim Cowan looked at me in disbelief. He was probably hoping that right now the USS Enterprise was orbiting the Earth ready to beam both of us up. My mouth was dry as I said, 'I've brought something better. Nobody get the wrong idea. I'm going to reach into the bag here and bring something of interest out.'

I slid my hand in slowly and felt among the newspaper for the ingot. I drew it out slowly and placed it beside Kev. The effect was instantaneous and transforming. Everybody gawped at it. Something made me look down at my hand and I noticed that my palm was shiny and golden.

Chapter 8

I stared in disbelief at the inside of my hand. I had just been given the Golden Palm award for being the biggest fucking eejit on God's earth. The fucking Bumble must have switched the real ingot for a painted bar of lead. I was now sitting at a table with one of Glasgow's renowned psychopaths, a Rottweiler with a passion for testicles, a Russian whose patron saint was the Marquis de Sade and a thug with an itchy trigger-finger on a sawn-off shotgun. My sphincter muscles began to twitch.

Luckily for me they were all still mesmerized at the supposed treasure before them. Slowly I put my hand forward, palm down naturally, and lifted the bar back into the bag, all eyes followed my action. I thought attack was probably the best form of defence. I applied the second rule of negotiation – self preservation.

'So Kev, you can have the goods here in exchange for Jim over there. You can sort out the rest with the Bumble yourself. How about it? There must be quite a few grand's worth of gold here.' I pushed my chair back and slowly got up. Tango gave a low growl of disapproval.

'Kev?' I said again and he looked up from the bag.

'Leave the Webley,' he said, 'I'll look forward to trying it out – like now.'

I was reaching for it when the guy with the sawn-off shouted, 'Dinnae even think about it!'

Kev picked it up and pointed it in my direction. 'Naebody walks in here and threatens me or my staff!' He lowered the gun, opened it and emptied out the brass shells. Then without even looking he replaced one and spun the cylinder.

'Bring our other friend over here.'

The Russian pushed Jim Cowan towards Kev. 'Sit him here.' Kev pulled back a chair, 'now blindfold him.'

'C'mon Kev,' I said. 'He's done you no harm.'

One of the thugs offered their Celtic scarf. The Russian tied it round Jim's eyes.

'The game begins,' said Kev and placed the barrel against Jim Cowan's temple. Jim began to shake and cry. Kev pulled the trigger. The hammer action clicked. Silence. 'Please, dear God I dinnae want to die...' Jim whimpered.

'Kev,' I said, 'your beef is with me, c'mon let him go.'

Kev pulled the trigger again. A dark patch appeared on Jim Cowan's trousers round his crotch.

'Jesus,' I muttered.

Kev laughed, Tango barked. 'Will we see if it's lucky number three?'

'That's enough Kev!' I moved forward to grab his arm. He levelled the gun at me. There was a sharp blast from the muzzle. Time went into slow motion.

'He's still standing,' said a voice.

I looked down at my midriff; sure enough I was in one piece.

Kev stared up, dumbfounded that I had not been blown in two. He placed the gun on the table, reached for another cartridge and held it up – there was no lead bullet attached to the end of it. Kev scoured the rest and then laughed, louder than I had ever heard him before. Tango and the rest of his entourage joined him. 'They're fucking blanks! Christ I never even noticed!' Tears ran down his face. 'Fucking good one! Best laugh I've had in years!'

I attempted to wake myself from the shock that I was still alive.

'Man,' said Kev, 'you're priceless! Strolling in here with blanks!'

There were hoots of derision all round as I patted my stomach for confirmation and checked that I hadn't soiled myself.

'Fucking priceless!' said Kev and again roared with laughter.

Recovering my nerve a little I said, 'I'm going to take Jim here.'

'Ah Christ!' said Kev. 'Ah that was good, aye, sure, fuck off and take that piece of shit with you. It'll be cheaper in the long run, considering the amount of grub he can shift down his neck. Aye go on and beat it! But mind you tell the Bumble I'll be coming for the rest of it. You and I will sort matters out another time.' He laughed again and shouted, 'Ho! Mick! Get out the twenty year old whisky again. Drinks all round boys.' A cheer went up.

I motioned with my eyes for Jim Cowan to move towards the exit and started to walk out backwards, trying not to show any sign of panic on my face.

When the Bumble's brother opened the pub door, in walked this wee old wifey dressed in a Salvation Army uniform. '*War Cry*, son?' she said.

I stared at her in disbelief, then put my hand into my pocket and pulled out a fiver.

'Here Sister,' I said stuffing it into her collecting can. 'The lads over there have just had a big win by the way.'

'On the dugs no doubt.'

'Something like that.' I pointed her in the direction of the Hole in the Wall gang gathered round the table.

'God Bless, son,' she said and strode forward with a zealot's purpose.

God be damned, I thought. If Kev noticed the gold wasn't for real the shit would really hit the fan and she would be the first in line if the hound was released – a dog always attacks the first thing in its path. It was at that moment that Kev held the fake gold ingot up to the light.

'My Gawd!' cried the Sally Ann wifey, like Saul on the road to Damascus. 'It must have been some dug to win ye all that.'

Kev looked up at her and placed the metal block back on the table. 'Aye Sister, whit dae ye want?'

She stuttered a barely audible, 'Copy of the *War Cry*?' and stared at the glittering object.

'Hey Mick, give the pilgrim here a ten spot from the till.'

I couldn't help but watch as Kev acted even more benevolently and stroked Tango. The mutt now had a gold streak on its head, which made it look like an upmarket skunk. There was a moment when I nearly broke into laughter but it left us as I opened the bar door and felt the cold air. Snow was falling. 'Okay?' I said to the Bumble's brother and then added, 'Run like fuck!'

We both legged it along the street not daring to look back lest, like Lot's wife, we would be turned into pillars of salt – along with the addition of ground beef. A few moments later we both stood gasping in the comparative safety of a busy city centre street. Passers-by studied us with inquisitive looks.

Flagging down a taxi, we bundled ourselves in and savoured the blast of warm air from the heater. I turned to Jim Cowan. 'You okay?' He nodded. 'Look,' I said, 'I don't think it's wise to go near the Bumble's office or head back to your flat in Edinburgh, so I want you to find an hotel out the west end. Call Davie once you find a place and let him know where you are. Here's one of his cards. We'll catch up later, okay?'

He nodded again. 'Thanks,' he muttered. 'I didn't think anyone was going to save me – I really thought I was going to die.'

'You and me both,' I said quietly, 'you and me both.'

I brought out the roll of cash the Bumble had given us and peeled off a couple of hundred. 'That should be enough to pay in advance for somewhere decent tonight and get some fresh clothes. Stay out the west end of the city, you should be fine there. Besides Kev isn't really interested in you. What about staying with your sister?'

'Linda?'

'Aye.'

He shook his head. 'No, I'll find a place and be in touch.'

I told the taxi driver to pull over at the far end of Argyle Street. I got out and said *adios*. The snow was still falling. One thing I had decided, the Bumble was a dead man. I decided to phone to see if the snake in the grass was in. If so, I was bringing my lawn mower.

I found a phone box and dialled his number. While it rang I got out my fags and lit one up with shaking fingers. The rest of me was still numb with shock. Behind me an old fella in a black duffel coat and wearing a red Santa hat played a tin whistle to the tune of *Jingle Bells*. The phone connected. 'Davie?' Nobody spoke. 'Davie, is that you, you bastard?' Still nobody answered.

The tin whistle echoed and I heard myself singing in my head, *Jingle Bells, Jingle Bells, jingle all the way* just as the answering machine picked up, followed by a brief ramble by the Bumble, then the usual bleep. I knew something wasn't right when a familiar but unplaceable male voice cut in. 'Hello?' I said nothing. 'Hello!'

I let the silence continue for a moment and then decided to reply. 'Aye, is Davie about?'

'No, I'm afraid not, can I take a message?'

I hung up. Either the Bumble had hired himself an efficient male secretary or there was a polite burglar at his office. I ruled out the former and since he had fuck all worth stealing at his office, I dismissed the latter. It was the voice though, that began to nag me. It sure wasn't Kev Barr or any of his mob but it made me feel uneasy. I stood staring at the crushed fag packet on top of the phone while the tin whistle player now gave his version of *The Snowman*. I smiled grimly to myself as it hit me. The voice belonged to Wilde, no, not Oscar, but Detective Chief Inspector Wilde, the Bumble's other sleeping partner.

I reckoned Wilde's visit to the Bumble's office wasn't a social call. And where was the fat bastard himself? I tried the Bumble's mobile and then his flat but there wasn't any reply from either. This was puzzling.

I called Charlie McLeod and asked him to meet me outside the office as soon as possible and to keep a sharp lookout for any of Kev Barr's mob. I reckoned it would be safe enough to visit the Bumble's lair with Wilde hanging about the place. Like a cat, curiosity was getting the better of me.

Taking out some more change, I strolled across to the old whistle player in the shop doorway and dropped it into his polystyrene cup. He gave us a nod and jauntily carried on, oblivious to the weather. Momentarily, I considered asking him if he would play *The Sash*.

I carried on walking along the street. Cars slithered and people scurried back and forth on personal missions, despite the conditions. As I approached Jamaica Street I noticed a police patrol car parked outside the Bumble's office. There was no sign of Charlie yet. Somehow I couldn't resist going up on my own. Besides, I wanted to see if the Bumble was there and if so, what was Wilde doing answering his phone.

Wiping snow from my jacket I was greeted by a uniformed plod stamping his feet at the entrance. 'Unless you live here pal,' he said barring my way, 'you can't come in.'

'I'm here to see DCI Wilde,' I said casually and took out a fresh packet of cigs. I lit one and he backed off since he wasn't too sure who I was. 'Told me to meet him here.' I gave him a short stare. He nodded and I headed up to the second floor.

'Where's Wilde?' I said to the cop guarding the office door.

'He's in the bog,' he said and nodded towards the end of the corridor. I peered in to see a white overalls team in the main office searching the place. This was getting stranger by the minute.

'So what gives?' I said taking a draw.

'They think the private dick that works from here is up at the city morgue. They found him in the Clyde, or what was left of him... they still have'nae found his head.'

Christ! I could'nae believe it. The Bumble dead! But I had only left him an hour or so ago. Kev Barr's mob couldn't have got to him that quickly, and besides, considering the con he pulled he would be expecting trouble.

'They hauled him out of the river?' I said inhaling even deeper on my cigarette.

'Aye, they reckon a boat's propeller done the damage. All they found on the body was his driving licence and a membership for a massage parlour up at Park Circus.'

We both looked round as the toilet flushed. The bolt slid back and Detective Chief Inspector Wilde stepped out. An evil stench followed.

Wilde was a short muscular guy of about late forties with unnatural black hair that sat atop his broad head like a racing yacht going full pelt. His dark saucer eyes gave signs of instant recognition.

'What the fuck are you doing here?' he said pulling on a navy blue woollen overcoat and tucking a red tartan scarf around the collar. The constable made himself scarce. 'Life not seedy enough for you?'

'Heard the Bumble had an extra workload, thought I might get a bit of seasonal employment with Christmas coming up, you know how it is.' I smiled longer than was polite.

'Always the smart ass, eh? Well listen, Sunny Jim, this might be a double murder enquiry, so don't go getting mixed up with anything connected to the Bumble... understand!'

He blew his nose into a grey hanky that might once have been white, and then surveyed the contents.

'That a threat?' I said.

'No, just good advice.'

'I'm touched,' I said, 'that someone as important as you should show concern for a lowly former colleague. I hear you still haven't found his head.'

'How do you know about that?' he said pushing the snotty hanky into his coat pocket.

I nodded towards the uniformed cop.

'Fucking typical woodentops,' he said loudly, but the guy just stood there looking blank as though he was listening to the snow falling.

'So, you really think the Bumble is stoking the fires of Hell?' I said.

'Maybe,' he replied. 'I suppose you can vouch for your movements in the last twenty four hours?'

'What makes you think I'd kill him?'

'The old statistic that most murdered people are killed by someone they know... and you work for him apparently. So what have you been up to recently?'

'Sleeping and Christmas shopping,' I said.

'Got anybody to corroborate your alibi? Preferably somebody not from the criminal classes.'

I watched the plods in the background searching the place and then glanced at my watch.

Wilde sneezed.

'*Gesundheit,*' I said.

Wilde blew loudly into his hanky again just as one of the forensic guys announced that the place was as clean as a whistle, there being no evidence of foul play having befallen the Bumble within his office.

'Then go over it again!' yelled Wilde.

I could feel the heat of his catarrh breath on my face as he said, 'I'll be talking to you again. Savvy?'

'Whatever you say boss,' I studied the mucus encrusted nasal hairs that protruded beyond his nostrils.

'Now beat it!' Wilde turned and closed the office door in my face.

Chapter 9

I suppose I always half expected the Bumble to come to an unsavoury end – aye, the Bumble's end, a bit more interesting than Howard's. In reality I wasn't so sure that he was dead – like Elvis I suppose. Though I didn't expect to find the Bumble behind the counter at Burger King on Argyle Street, nor did I expect a religious cult to grow up around him like the Presleyterians. The First Bumbleterian Church of God didn't have a ring of salvation about it.

There was little to be gained from hanging about his office and besides Wilde and his lads were ripping the place apart – for what, I really didn't know because the Bumble wouldn't leave anything of value in the joint, certainly not gold or the documents. And apparently there was no evidence that he had been killed there. It was probably Wilde venting his wrath on the Bumble for not producing the goods.

As I came out of the dimly lit close, I saw Charlie in the Capri. I approached his car and noticed a large grim faced goon watching me from behind the wheel of a grimy white Transit van on the other side of the road. There was too much heat about for him to do anything so I smiled and gave him the finger. I opened the door of the Capri and got in.

'We're being watched by the way,' I said and Charlie glanced up from reading the early edition of the Evening Times.

'That's Second Prize McLennan behind the wheel,' he said. 'Any brains he had have long since been punched out of him. Never won a fight in his life.'

'Does he work for Kev Barr?'

Charlie nodded. 'One of his strong arm boys. The van is probably packed with muscle and baseball bats.'

'Think they'll cause trouble?'

'Doubt it, too much heat around. Probably just curious the same as I am. What's going on up at the Bumble's palace?' He folded up the paper and unwrapped a treacle toffee.

'Chief Inspector Wilde thinks the Bumble is dead, headless to be precise. Found some remains in the Clyde and he thinks they're his.'

Charlie chewed on his confectionery for a moment or two without a hint of concern for the Bumble's demise. 'You believe Wilde?'

'Frankly? Not a lot, considering I left the Bumble a couple of hours ago in good health.' I opened the glove compartment and took the half-bottle of whisky out. 'Mind you, I did warn him about where he was putting his pecker, but I doubt it was a jealous husband. Come on let's get out of here and I'll give you an update on the proceedings.' I took several slugs from the bottle as Charlie coaxed the Capri along the slush and into the traffic.

The man in the van attempted to follow but we eventually lost him. We headed over to Hillhead, a semi-respectable part of the city.

'You had lunch?' said Charlie.

'No,' I said with a shiver.

We parked up and made for the Curlers pub with its mainly student clientele. I bought a couple of pints of lager while Charlie scanned the chalked menu on the blackboard. 'Steak pie sounds just about right,' he said, 'had enough of Turkey dinners already.'

I nodded approval.

We took a seat. Charlie wiped the froth from his moustache. 'You were going to give me an update.'

I recounted all that I had been through and also the Bumble's theory on Rudolf Hess.

Charlie was to the point. 'Stupid fucker!'

'The Bumble?'

'No, you. Walking into Kev Barr's pub like that with a firearm – that was asking for it.'

'It was the Bumble's fault,' I protested like a guilt ridden teenager to a parent, 'he set me up.'

'Fuck him. You should know better than that. Christ! You could have called me.'

'Wasn't thinking.'

'No you weren't,' he said, 'and as far as the bar of gold goes... if its real... it dis'nae constitute the hidden hoards of the Third Reich.'

'I was convinced the Bumble stumbled on to something.'

'The Bumble's *always* onto something – you should know that.'

'Aye, I know,' I said taking a sip of lager, 'but I've seen a photograph of Mrs Van Luben with a young German flyer.'

'All I'm trying to tell you,' replied Charlie, 'is not to believe all you hear or see. Most of Glasgow knew the rumours about Van Luben. It was like he was an urban myth. You know, like the rat they found in the fried chicken take-away, covered in the secret recipe.'

We sat back to allow a friendly young blonde waitress to place down our food.

'But what about Tony McCaffrey?' I said breaking the piecrust and letting the savoury steam escape. I speared a cube of beef.

'What about him?' said Charlie digging into his own pie, 'He could have died having a toss with a rope around his neck – it's called auto-erotic asphyxiation.'

'You didn't see the marks on his arms and legs.'

'But you found evidence of Tony's predilection for bondage magazines. He was possibly into such things. Christ, he could have been at it with anybody! Even Jim Cowan.'

'Now you're just being homophobic. Was Tony gay?'

'How the fuck would I know?'

'You know Linda quite well.'

'What's that supposed to mean?'

'Nothing.' I fumbled for my cigs.

'Look,' said Charlie unfastening his jacket, 'people get up to all sorts of things behind closed doors – all I'm saying is it's not beyond the realms of possibility and that's the way the cops are going to see it. Unless the autopsy turns up anything different. That bampot Barr and the Russian probably just showed up at the same time as yourself and tried to scare you for old time's sake. Look at what happened today.'

'I suppose.'

For several minutes we concentrated on our steak pies, spuds and veg. Charlie finally mashed his potatoes into the gravy, soaking up the last rich dark drops while I mopped my plate with bread.

'Not bad,' he said, 'not bad at all.' He carefully dabbed his whiskers again with a serviette.

I nodded. 'Yeah, pretty good.' The cheerful waitress appeared from the wings, enquiring if we wanted anything from the dessert list. Charlie patted his broad stomach and declined. 'You're okay doll, trying to keep my boyish figure.'

She glanced in my direction. 'No thanks sweetheart.'

'I hope Jim Cowan is okay,' I went on, draining the contents of my glass.

'Look,' said Charlie, 'the Bumble's brother is an eejit and I'm not being prejudiced in any way. Take it from me, if he hadn't allowed that toerag McCaffrey to stay with him then he wouldn't have got dragged into anything. Right now the best thing he could do is hand himself in to the police and assist them with their enquiries. Unless he's got something to hide?'

'Don't know... don't think so. I'm pretty sure he's just a hapless victim in all this.'

'No such thing,' said Charlie and stretched. 'Remember the majority of murdered people are killed by those they know – fact.'

'Yeah, yeah, Wilde just gave me the same lecture. I'm getting the picture.'

Charlie got up to go to the bar. I pondered where the Bumble could be – apart from in the city morgue.

'Cheers,' I said as Charlie placed a couple of fresh pints on the table. 'So what about the Bumble?'

'He'll turn up – I'm convinced of it. Don't worry, I'm pretty sure whoever it is up the morgue, it ain't him. Listen I'll have a word with some of the lads at Police HQ over on Pitt Street. Okay?'

I nodded, took a sip of lager and felt for my cigarettes again.

'What's your plans for Christmas then?' said Charlie.

'Haven't really thought about it, to tell you the truth. More concerned about staying alive.'

'Relax, Kev has to watch over his own shoulder these days. He's got an ambitious son. You know him, Malkie Barr, aka the Malkie Barr Kid.

'What? He was in short pants the last time I saw him.'

'That was at least fifteen years ago, he's all grown up and a real chip of the old block.'

I reached into my shirt pocket and brought out some cash to pay for the meal.

'Give it to charity,' said Charlie, 'my shout.'

'Sure?'

'Sure. Oh and there's something I forgot to tell you... Linda called me wanting to speak to you. No doubt about Tony. Look, do her and yourself a favour. Go and tell her that you found nothing suspicious about his death. Let the cops reveal things – if as I said there's anything to be found. Okay, it may be difficult to grasp that given the circumstances... you know what I'm trying to say? I know it must be hard for her to take it in that her son was found hanged, but it happens.'

'She didn't seem that upset the other night at the party.'

Charlie shrugged his shoulders, 'She's a tough cookie, a survivor.'

'I'll call her later,' I said playing with a cig between my fingers. 'What are you up to now?'

'Got a couple of clients to see. They're up in court soon, so I need statements from them. They're as guilty as hell.'

I sparked up my cigarette

Charlie picked up the bill. 'Keep an eye over your shoulder meantime and give me a buzz later.'

'Will do,' I said firmly snapping the Zippo shut and slid a couple of quid under the plate for the waitress.

Chapter 10

Curiosity still whispered away about the whole episode involving the Bumble and his theory on Rudolf Hess. Something nagged at me that there might be an element of truth in it somewhere. I thought a little bit of research of my own might help, so I decided to visit the militaria dealer who had told Kev Barr about the documents. I just couldn't resist taking a poke into his bunker. From what I remembered the guy was out the far end of Dumbarton Road, so that's where I headed.

I found his shop without too much trouble. It was called the 'Pill Box'. Standing outside I gave the window a look over. The display was largely made up of faded red, white and blue British Union flags, some assorted sepia postcards, military badges and a few medals. The centrepiece of the display was an old Royal Navy poster that featured a bearded Jolly Jack tar with a welcoming hand. The advertisement asked for smart young men to *Join and feel a man* – some things never change.

From the outside it didn't look too nefarious, so I pushed the door and went in. An old brass overhead bell attached to a spring tinkled to announce my presence. It was dim and smelled of stale tobacco and dampness. The joint was packed with glass cabinets full of helmets, uniforms, bayonets, medals

– but it was the Third Reich display that got me. There were mannequins in full black SS uniforms with backdrops of swastika flags and a portrait of the Führer, which looked as though some kid had done it with a painting by numbers set.

'Can I help you mate?' said this low pitched male voice emanating from a figure half hidden by a black curtain in what was presumably the back shop. A small bald headed guy in his late thirties with a gingerish beard stepped out. He was definitely not a specimen of the master race. I thought of asking if Deputy Führer Hess was about but decided to play simple.

'Naw, you're okay thanks,' I said and continued to look around the grotto. What I was hoping to find I don't know.

'Collect anything in particular?' he asked.

I scratched my chin. 'Gold, Nazi gold.'

He frowned with suspicion, not knowing where I was coming from.

'If I had some I would'nae be here,' he said in a nervous tone and chuckled.

'Too bad,' I said, 'I was hoping we could do some business.'

There was a light cough from the back shop. He wasn't alone.

I scanned some more of the cabinets, feigning interest.

'Maybe,' I said 'we could have a chat later.'

'I don't think so – now if you'll excuse me I'm going to have to close.'

'I could make it worth your while.'

He didn't respond.

'If you change your mind give me a call.' I handed him one of the Bumble's business cards. He gave it a glance, and as I opened the shop door I paused for a second. 'Have a merry Christmas,' I said, 'Oh, by the way, everybody that's come in contact with those documents you told Kev Barr about has wound up dead.' I enjoyed rattling him. Besides it was the season of good will. The bell resounded again with a tinkle as I yanked the door shut.

I was lucky there was a greasy spoon cafe across the road called Maria's – least that's what the sign said. I hacked my way through the fug and ordered a coffee. Picking up a copy of the Glasgow Herald from the rack at the end of the counter I sat in a window booth that had a reasonable view of the militaria shop.

I scanned the paper, checking out the births, deaths and marriages in the off chance I might know someone. Taking a sip of coffee I glanced across the road at the shop. Nobody had come out and nobody gone in. I resumed my interest in the latest city news. A local boxer, Earl Lanagan, 28, had been fined £150 for being pished and causing an affray at a night club in the city. Maybe he'd been punch drunk.

I stirred the froth on the coffee and added an extra sugar lump. Then, just as I was about to resume my interest in the paper the militaria shop proprietor came out. An old white haired bloke in a dark blue anorak accompanied him. Maybe it was his father. The dealer craned his neck left and right no doubt checking if I was still hanging about while his elderly companion glanced at the heavy laden sky. For a moment I thought he looked familiar. I watched them saunter along the street a few yards and then get into a black BMW saloon. There seemed nothing remarkable about either of them – but that was to underestimate unremarkable people the world over. I noted the registration number and lit a fresh cigarette.

I wasn't in a hurry so I ordered another white coffee and resumed my interest in the local rag while I thought of Linda, the Bumble's sister, and what I was going to tell her. *Your son? He had a peaceful air about him, I'm sure he's in a better place. A terrible accident, I'm really sorry.* There's never an easy option.

There was a payphone at the back of the cafe so I called her. She sounded tired, but was happy to see me later. I again offered my condolences without any further comment. I called Charlie on his mobile to see if he had heard any developments on the Bumble.

'It's not him up at the morgue,' he said unless he's lost about 150lbs in weight since yesterday,' he paused. 'It's a pick-pocket, Tijuana McCormack. Do you remember him? Lived out at Govan Cross.'

'The amputee guy? Had his false arm weighted with lead for mugging folk? The original one armed bandit?'

'Aye,' said Charlie, 'the one and the same. They found his head. Seems he's dipped his last pocket with the Bumble's wallet. The Polis have got witnesses who saw an incident down at the Broomielaw. Some guy beat the crap out of Tijuana with his false arm and pushed him into the river. A passing boat done the rest. Churned him up with the propeller.'

I'm sure there was a moral in the tale somewhere.

'Could you check out a licence plate for me?' I said and gave him the number from the militaria dealer's BMW.

'Listen I have to go, catch you later,' said Charlie and the line went dead.

I smiled, so the fat bastard was alive. In a way I was relieved, happy to hear that he was still on this mortal coil.

'Good news?' inquired the café assistant as he placed my coffee beside me on a shelf beside the phone.

'For some,' I said and thanked him.

Eventually I headed back home keeping a watchful eye for a welcoming committee. The hot water felt good as I showered. The grime and tiredness began to fade. I shaved and dressed and had a quick bowl of Heinz oxtail soup while watching the evening news followed by an inane soap about village life, then called a taxi and headed for my date with the Marmalade Cat.

Chapter 11

'Nice to see you,' she said as the door swung open at 31 St Margaret's Drive, an expensive Victorian villa in a desirable postcode area of Glasgow's well to do west end. She smiled with sunset red lips. 'Give me your coat... come on in and have a drink.' I caught a whiff of heady perfume.

I studied her more than pleasant figure as she hoisted my jacket onto a peg. We ascended the stairs together in silence and then she ushered me into the lounge. The cream leather settees looked ultra comfortable as she gestured to take a seat. Flames licked away from the coals in a white marble fireplace. I briefly watched a pendulum swinging back and forth on an old wall-mounted mahogany clock in the far corner.

'Lovely place you have,' I said.

'Drink?'

'Thanks.'

'Brandy? It's a cold night after all,' she said.

The Bumble's sister had done all right for herself. She could hardly miss though, marrying Frank McCaffrey, who ran various rackets around the city – until he dropped dead from a heart attack a few years back. Yep, the Bumble's family knew a good catch when they saw one.

The Marmalade Cat handed me a large measure in a cut crystal glass.

'Cheers,' she said and our glasses clinked, 'and a Merry Christmas.' She was optimistic at least.

Sitting opposite me on the matching sofa, she placed her drink on a coaster and opened a worked copper art nouveau cigarette box. 'Help yourself,' she said.

'Thanks,' I said and lifted a gold-banded Dunhill out of the box. I eyed her cleavage as she too leaned forward for a cigarette. I pondered on the possibility of having sex with her. Maybe, like herself, I was just trying to confirm that I was still alive after recent events. Stretching over I offered a light. She blew the smoke upwards at the ornate ceiling features. The Cherubs looked on.

'So,' she said.

I didn't need any further prompts and decided to get the worst of the evening out the way. I took a large slug of brandy. 'It seems Tony got mixed up with a shady bastard by the name of Kev Barr. Heard of him?'

She nodded and took a sip of her drink. 'Do you think he killed Tony?'

'Possibly,' I said, deciding to keep the part about the Nazi documents out of my story. 'Look, let's be honest about your son, he wasn't a saint and if you get mixed up with people like Kev Barr... well it sort of goes with the territory.' I was going to say *like father like son* but thought better of it. I finished the remains in my glass quickly.

'So that makes it alright?' she said, drawing deeply on her cigarette.

'No,' I said, 'I'm sorry, I didn't mean to be brutal about things.'

'You're right anyway,' she said. 'I don't know what I was expecting.' She kicked off her pink mules and drew her knees up onto the settee. I noticed her bare feet and the bright red nail varnish adorning her toenails.

I got up and poured another couple of brandies and sat down beside her. She began to cry. It was probably the first time she had properly grieved for Tony.

'I'm sorry, I don't know what's come over me,' she said, wiping her eyes with a tissue. I wanted to take her there and then – despite the fact she was a relative of the Bumble.

'Listen,' I said reaching forward to catch a tear on her cheek, 'I don't know if I can give you the truth about Tony, maybe we'll never know what happened...' I didn't say any more. The rest of the tale would only cloud the already murky water.

'I had you figured out right,' she said with a smile and gently touched my shoulder. 'You're not like the rest of them.' She took a large gulp of brandy. 'Anyway, thanks for being honest about my step-son.'

'Stepson? I didn't realise...' I said.

'He was from Frank's first marriage, I never had any children of my own.'

She leaned forward and kissed me. I felt the stallion below rising to the occasion.

I stared at her a bit longer than I should have, but I couldn't help it. She sat back and pushed her hair from her face, giving me a soft inviting smile. I took a slow draw on my cig and then, instead of unleashing the forces of desire I heard myself saying: 'I don't suppose you've heard from Davie recently have you?' I sipped some more brandy. 'Only he seems to have vanished.'

The Marmalade Cat looked surprised at the question, quite clearly not expecting any further conversation. 'He called about half an hour ago... just before you arrived.'

'D'you know where he is?' I said eagerly.

'I'm sure he said he was down at that office of his catching up on some paperwork.'

I stubbed my cigarette out. 'Look, this is important, Linda, I'll have to go. I'm sorry. I'll be in touch.'

She looked bewildered and taken aback as I grabbed my coat and left. I didn't want to call him. Re-unions are so much better when they're a surprise. A full moon illuminated the sky as I headed down towards the underground at Kelvinbridge to catch the Clockwork Orange for St Enoch's station.

Half an hour later I was standing outside the Bumble's office looking for any sign of malevolent presence. Traffic passed by with the odd car pulling in to discuss terms with the working girls. There was no sign of gorillas in vans. I studied the office window but it was in darkness. I couldn't believe the bastard was still up there but I thought I'd better take a look-see.

The stairwell light shone with a dull glow that reflected off the faded blue paint that had once adorned the walls. I made my way up to the second floor paying attention to the worn steps. The landing for the Bumble's office was in darkness, so I got out my lighter, ran my thumb down the striker and held the flickering flame up to see my way towards his office door. I felt like a tomb robber.

The plods had put a piece of plastic tape across it, saying: *Police Do not Cross*. I held the flame under it and watched it shrivel. The door locks had been changed. I took a step back and lurched forward with my shoulder. There was a splintering of wood as the frame gave way. I looked round to see if anybody was going to respond but it seemed all quiet, so I went in and closed the door behind me. I felt for a light switch and gave it a flick to illuminate the outer office. The place was cold and damp. There was definitely no sign of the Bumble.

I sparked up a cigarette and wandered through to our centre of operations. What I was looking for, I didn't quite know, beyond hoping that the bastard was hiding in a cupboard and somebody had left a big fucking stick for me to beat the shit out of him with. Something wasn't right I could sense it.

I know Wilde had searched the place with the proverbial fine-tooth comb but I figured there was no harm in having another look see. Opening the grey filing cabinet I had a rummage through it. The files were mainly for cases related to divorce and people who were swinging the lead while off on the sick. I suppose Wilde didn't consider them important enough to take with him. I'd thought I'd try the desk drawers but they were empty, save for a couple of phone directories and a copy of *Razzle* – a magazine that featured large breasted ladies. There was no sign of the whisky. Wilde and his crew must have nicked it.

I pulled the desk drawers out and turned them upside down, I knew it was unlikely there would be anything there and sure enough there was fuck all. Looking down at the linoleum I wondered if it was worth lifting. I could well be eaten by the wildlife that lived on it but figured it was worth a try. It peeled back with a tacky feel, to reveal nothing more than a few old copies of the Daily Record and the Glasgow Herald. I shivered and went to see if the kettle had been left in the cupboard. I was in luck.

Five minutes later I had brewed up a cup of black tea. The warmth was welcome as I wrapped my hands round a cracked white mug. I peeled back some more of the lino but it was just the same assortment of old newspapers. Picking a few of them up just to see what was going on in yesteryears, I read as I sipped my warm beverage. One paper featured the Moon landing, others the arse the Americans were making of Vietnam. Mind you, a fortnight in Spain was only fifty quid then. There didn't seem like anything of interest though. I sighed, placed my mug down on top of one of the papers, and there, right in front of me was an article about a Glasgow car dealer by the name of Van Luben. There was a photograph of some sort of celebration. Van Luben was in the centre of it, surrounded by others offering him a toast.

I couldn't believe it. It was the fucking fleeing Dutchman. I sat at the desk and read the article. It was dated the 20th April 1969 and Van Luben had been celebrating twenty years of success in Glasgow. The date sounded familiar for some reason. The Bumble had been smart; I'll give him that. Nobody had seen the obvious lying in front of them. I tore round the area of interest and put it in my inside coat pocket for a closer inspection later on.

The cold and the tea were beginning to stretch my bladder so I headed for the bog down the hall. I was standing there feeling a sense of relief, when I smelled something that wasn't from the old pink air freshener or the drains. It was petrol. Zipping up, I turned to open the toilet door and there was a quiet whooshing as the hallway lit up with a fierce brightness. The place was getting fucking torched! Flames licked the walls as I ran down the hall towards the main door. Getting kebabbed in this hole was not my idea of a final farewell.

By the time I was out on the landing smoke was pouring out of the Bumble's office. I couldn't see anybody but I noticed a light filtering out from a neighbouring door a few feet away. I thumped on it. A few moments later an elderly man, with an unnaturally dark Clarke Gable moustache, peered out from a chained door. He held a nervous blonde Alsatian on a lead beside him. The dog looked well pissed off at having got dragged along to potentially savage anybody intent on having a go at his master.

'Whit do ye want?' he said, 'I'll let ma dug loose if ye dinnae clear off.'

'The building's on fire Pops, let's get out of here!'

'Ah'm going nowhere, this is ma hame. Now if you don't clear aff...' The old guy never finished his sentence as the glass on the Bumble's office door shattered and flames roared out like a beast in search of prey.

'Come on!' I said, 'Get out!'

He undid the chain and stood there frozen with fear.

'Get down those stairs.' I grabbed him by the collar, shoving him forward. 'Anybody else on this level?'

'Naw, I'm the last private resident on this floor – ma dug, ma dug it won't move!'

The heat was getting fiercer by the second. I looked at the dog and the dog looked at me. It wagged its tail then began to piss on the carpet.

'Who's a good girl then?' I said in a deceptively soft tone. The dog just cowered, so I bent down, picked it up and carried it. Its master shuffled along beside me. I took one last glance at the inferno as the smoke and flames swept along then made for the stairs. 'Fire!' I shouted as we hurried down. Several doors opened and a few more tenants clattered out with us.

I was never so glad to get down the stairs and out into the street. Gently I placed the dog down and it relieved itself. A cloud of steam rose into the cold night air. A small crowd gathered, while the old man repeatedly mourned his home, 'All I have is up there,' he said, 'whit am I going tae do now?' I didn't have much to offer him other than a cigarette.

Windows to the frontage of the building cracked violently and a shower of glass fell at our feet. Everybody hopped back.

I lit my own cigarette and disappeared into the night before the authorities turned up to ask questions. That could keep until tomorrow.

Chapter 12

As I walked away from the crowd I couldn't help but think that God does not save us from hard times – hard times come to believers and non-believers alike. Right now it was my turn for a generous helping from the bowels of misfortune. Death was definitely stalking me.

A fire engine raced past us towards the Bumble's office. Shit happens, but it was happening with alarming regularity.

I pondered who had tried to torch me. The odds on favourite I suppose, was Kev Barr. Maybe he had someone watching the place that I hadn't seen, maybe one of the local ladies of the street short on trade and keen to have a Christmas bonus. I discounted that theory because Kev Barr would have also issued the order for a kicking and dowsed me with petrol for good measure. I flagged down a taxi and started with the person who told me the Bumble had called from his office – the Marmalade Cat.

'Where to pal?' said the bespectacled driver.

I looked at his broken nose, ragged ears and eyes that told you not to fuck with him – despite being behind glasses. I gave him Linda McCaffrey's address.

'Bit of a bonfire back there,' he said glancing into the rear view mirror.

'Aye,' I replied watching the reflection of the orange flames in the taxi window.

'Did'nae realise that anybody still stayed in those old rat holes. A disgrace, a fucking disgrace, pardon the French pal, but it's so typical, the money gets spent on the city centre but half a mile away in any direction...'

My thoughts were elsewhere as he began to rabbit on about social depravation and the rights of man – that's one thing about Glasgow taxi drivers they're always knowledgeable about political discourse and ready to jump on the barricades. Aye, I was being driven through the streets of Glasgow by fucking Citizen Robespierre. I hoped he was towing a mobile guillotine because a few heads were going to come off if I had my way.

By the time we got to Kelvinside he had moved on to the subject of football and the piss poor performance of the Rangers.

'Fuckin disgrace, that's an eejit in charge at Ibrox. The Celtic are running rings round us...' he said, narrowly missing an old wifey at a crossing.

I don't suppose he was in the mood to hear about the remix version of *The Sash* that he could buy over at the Barras market. We drew up outside Linda McCaffrey's residence. The lights were on – I hoped somebody was at home.

'This it here pal? I can see better now since I got these new glasses. Helps the blindness in my right eye... good job you were on the left hand side of the street when you flagged us down.'

Brilliant, I had been driven around Glasgow by a one-eyed taxi driver whose nickname was probably Patch.

'Four pounds eighty mate,' he said through the glass partition. I handed him a fiver and told him to keep the change as twenty pence was about all his patter was worth. I got out, lit a cig and rang Linda McCaffrey's doorbell for the second time that night. A few seconds later I saw her looking down from the bay window then she disappeared until I saw her outline through the frosted glass inner door. She opened it.

'Hi, remember me? Or weren't you expecting me to rise from the ashes?'

She looked puzzled. 'Come in,' she said and gestured towards the stairs. We climbed them together yet again and went into the lounge. Without waiting to be asked I poured a large measure of brandy and took a mouthful.

'Didn't expect you to be back tonight,' she said and stared at me with her arms folded.

'No, I bet you didn't,' I replied and slugged back the entire contents of the glass.

'I don't know if I like your tone,' she said. 'Look, what's this all about? You went rushing out of here an hour ago and now you're back with an attitude.'

'You would have fucking attitude as well if your arse had almost been grilled.'

She looked slightly angry. 'Why don't you start again and tell me what this is all about and for fuck's sake sit down!'

I did as she asked while she took my empty glass and refilled it. If she was involved, she was acting pretty cool about the whole affair. I thanked her as she handed me another brandy and told her about my evening.

'And you think I set you up? Well thanks a lot,' she said.

'Wouldn't you' I replied'

'Why would I want to kill you?'

105

I guess she had a point.

'Listen,' she said, 'it's dreadful about his office and the old guy next door, but Davie deals with a lot of unsavoury people. Maybe it was one of them or maybe a property developer. You know what these people are like. Would you like something to eat? I had it ready for you when you first came round.'

I had to admit I was hungry. It must have been all that adrenaline.

'Linda, thanks, but I'm still concerned for Davie's safety. I can't get a hold of him, despite him calling you earlier.' I crushed out my cigarette.

She smiled and said, 'He's probably over at his latest girlfriend's flat. Mind you met her at the party? Priscilla?'

'Oh, aye, her, where does she stay?'

'Can't mind, out Partick direction I think'

'Got her phone number?' I asked.

'Sorry. Lets eat eh? Salmon okay? You do like a bit of fish?'

'Now and then,' I said.

The meal was good, especially when it was washed down with a crisp chilled French white wine. By now I had no intentions of running after any bastard, especially the Bumble. Linda sat opposite me cradling her glass.

I wondered if my prospects of sliding between the sheets with her were still on the cards. I decided to test the water.

'Time to go,' I said and stood up.

Linda remained seated on the settee. 'Must you?'

We gazed at each other in silence for a moment. Then I turned away to place my glass on the side table next to the settee. I was about to sit beside her when I saw something that made me freeze. On a table beside the settee was a collection of photographs in silver frames. One in particular caught my attention. A sharp-faced guy in a suit had his arm around Linda. I picked it up and studied it closely to make absolutely sure – it was Frank McCaffrey. He was also one of the punters in the newspaper article I had found under the lino at the Bumble's office. Then I looked at her. 'Your late husband, did he know Peter Van Luben?'

She pondered the question for a second. 'Frank knew a lot of people, he was a businessman.'

'You didn't answer my question.'

'Look, I've had enough for one night. I'm going to bed... alone! Now if you don't mind.' She got up and held the lounge door open.

Well, that killed any chance I had of sleeping in the wet patch. I finished my glass of wine and said, 'Thanks. I'll show myself out,' getting the hard stare that only women know how to do.

I consoled myself with the thought I'd wake alone but alive.

A cold wind blew as I stepped out into the night. I turned up my collar. *Bah fucking humbug!*

Chapter 13

I poured a large whisky when I got home and sat back in a comfy armchair watching the coal-effect gas fire burning with an even glow and was thankful I'd escaped the inferno that engulfed the Bumble's office. I also thought of the elderly gent with his dog and wondered where they were. It was turning out to be an eventful Christmas. I was tired though, tired of the whole affair not least because I seemed to be the mug, the sucker, the fall guy, the fucking eejit that you wind up and let loose to sniff around.

Sipping the malt I unfolded the newspaper from my inside jacket pocket. The line-up wouldn't have looked out of place in the Police Gazette. There was Van Luben and Frank McCaffrey beside an odd assortment of acquaintances. It was hard to believe that a hoodlum like McCaffrey supped with Nazis, but there again Fascism and greed had a wide appeal.

I lit a cig and studied the faces. One guy resembled a younger version of the old geezer I had seen coming out the militaria shop, but maybe that was just taking coincidence too far. I savoured a mouthful of spirit and let it slide down the gullet. There was just a chance that the Bumble's sister knew nothing about her husband's interests – like the German Nation when they were made aware of their atrocities she appeared to 'know nothing'. My eyelids felt heavy as I fought back tiredness. For a brief moment I thought about my Celtic Princess, Heather, and made a mental note to pay her a visit if the Cops, Kev Barr, Tango, the Glasgow Nazi Party and the lone nutter with a gallon of petrol didn't get me first.

No matter how hard I tried to sleep my mind just wouldn't relax. I scanned the bookcase at 1.25am to find something that would slip my mind into neutral. *The Kings Regulations 1914* didn't appeal nor the *Domesday Book*. I didn't fancy re-fighting the Somme or de-coding Napoleon's cyphers and settled on the obvious: *The Big Sleep*.

I awoke early and went for a stroll amid the early morning punters heading to work. It was cold; frost lay on the pavements and your breath was visible. I crossed the road to my local Cafe that was open for business. Even at the back of eight o'clock the place was busy. I savoured the greasy bacon roll smeared with ketchup and a mug of coffee. Several re-fills and another bacon roll later I felt ready to do a bit of research at the Mitchell reference library. I hopped the train and headed for the city centre.

By late morning I concluded one thing – Hess still had followers, as did his beloved Führer. Theories abounded around his last flight to Scotland – everything from grand conspiracies with sympathetic British aristocrats, to the belief that the Germans cunningly sent a doppelgänger in Hess's place.

I drew one conclusion from the relatively sane academic works – Hess's bum was out of the window with regard to his relationship with Adolf Hitler. It seems that in September 1939, Hitler relegated Hess from being Deputy Führer and gave the job to that fat bastard Herman Goring. On the war front, old Adolf was making preparations to invade Russia as early as July 1940. Hess wasn't a happy bunny about the thought of the old German military dilemma of war on two fronts – it hadn't worked for the Kaiser and his moustache so why should it work for Adolf's? Hess didn't share his beloved leader's optimism and had formulated an alternative plan by the autumn of 1940. He was an avid pilot and contacted his old friend Willi Messerschmitt to kit out a long range twin-engined plane for the job – an Me 110E. I pondered this fact wondering why he'd taken such a large plane and not a Me 109 single seat fighter equipped with extra fuel tanks that could have been discarded when empty. Of course he told his pal Willi that it was just for a spot of sightseeing – as you would.

Hess's plan came together in the late afternoon of the 10th of May 1941. He took off from Augsburg near Munich – fifty miles from the Swiss border and ninety from Zurich where, according to the document the Bumble had shown me, the gold had been withdrawn a few days beforehand.

He was probably an hour into his flight when Adolf Galland, the German fighter ace who commanded a squadron down on the northern French coast, received a telephone call from fat Herman. Goring ranted on that a leading Nazi had gone mad – which must have come as a complete surprise to Galland. Goring revealed that it was no less a figure than Rudolf Hess who had done a runner and that Galland was to intercept him and shoot him down. Galland, probably knowing Goring's propensity for drugs, in all likelihood thought Herman was on his own amphetamine-fuelled flight. Nevertheless, to oblige, he sent up a couple of fighters to appease the fat focker. Galland knew that even if it was true, it would be almost impossible to find Hess amid the other aircraft in a war zone and besides, even if he made it to Scotland, he would in all probability be shot down.

One thing did come across though, and that was the fact that Herman Goring knew about Hess legging it even before Hitler did. Adolf wasn't informed until the next morning. I had my own theory that it all revolved around thieves falling out. I couldn't prove the gold angle but it was entirely plausible. Maybe the truth lay somewhere in between. Hess allegedly desired peace, took it upon himself to propose it, but needed a bit of spending money in the event he would have a few years to while away in exile before there were any changes in Germany.

As it turned out, Hess spent the war banged up and was eventually trotted out at Nuremberg only to be incarcerated in Spandau for the rest of his natural – until he was found with an electrical flex around his neck. Some say it was suicide, while the Hess family claim it was murder – but there again, such intrigue always surrounded the Nazis. Or maybe, just maybe, somebody knew there was a pot of gold at the end of the rainbow and didn't want any loose ends.

I also discovered that April 20th was Adolf Hitler's birthday and that was what in all probability was being celebrated in the newspaper article I had about Van Luben.

I also needed to find the Bumble. Thanking the library staff for their assistance I left and found a phonebox. Charlie was receiving visitors. I decided to walk to his flat and enjoy some winter sunshine. All the shops were trying to flog overpriced Christmas crap while reminding you that only a few days remained for them to relieve you of your cash. I lit a cig as I walked and considered the permutations of who wanted what and why.

Wandering up the hill past the darkened gothic structure of the University I noticed a Santa Claus in traditional garb ringing a hand bell. Beside him was a red bucket that declared it was for the student Christmas welfare fund. Santa almost deafened me as he deliberately swung the bell past my left ear crying, 'Spare change for the needy!'

I took a last draw on my cig and dropped it into his bucket, then strolled on with a 'Ho, fucking Ho!'

Chapter 14

'That tea you're making?' I said as I entered Charlie's flat. I hung my jacket and scarf over a hook on the oak hall stand.

Charlie sighed and closed the main door. 'Ah suppose.'

Our footsteps echoed down the hallway when we hit a bare patch of waxed floorboard that didn't have coverage from one of the Persian rugs. I momentarily gazed up at the McLeod's assortment of washing on the overhead pulley in the kitchen. There was nothing out of the ordinary, no sensational underwear, just socks knickers and shirts in dark hues.

Charlie dumped the old tea bags from the ancient aluminium tea pot in the bin, scoured it out, poured some hot water into it, gave it a swirl and sloshed it into the sink.

'Christ man! You could die of thirst in here,' I said breaking into a fresh packet of cigs. 'You're like an old wifey at the tea making. You'll be reading the cups next.'

He ignored me and completed his alchemy.

'Anybody been looking for me?' I said, getting a couple of blue mugs off the shelf with Rangers FC insignia across them.

'No,' said Charlie pouring the brew, 'who of the many are you expecting?'

Portraits of Rangers legendary players appeared on the side of the mugs – they were heat reactive. I got Paul 'Gazza' Gascoigne.

'The Police.' I said and poured in milk. 'The Bumble's office got torched last night when I was having a rake around. I was lucky to get out alive and so was the old boy who lived a few doors along.'

Charlie halted the ascent of the mug towards his mouth and placed it back on the table.

'Let me get this straight. The Bumble's office went up in flames? He ain't going to be too pleased about that.'

'Never mind the fucking Bumble not being pleased, how do you think I feel? Yesterday I could have been shot or burned to death.'

'Sorry,' said Charlie and opened a packet of dark chocolate digestives.

I took a slurp of tea and reached for a biscuit.

'So someone put a match to it?' said Charlie.

'Do you think the Bumble burned his own office?' I said, spooning in more sugar.

'Why would he?' Charlie shrugged. 'It's not as if the place was worth much.'

'Were developers wanting the land?'

'Not that I've heard,' he said, 'but that's not to say it isn't possible.'

I lifted another biscuit. The phone rang and we looked at each other.

'Might be business,' said Charlie getting up to answer it, 'dinnae finish the packet.'

I could hear him uttering a few 'aye's and 'if you want to, and a final 'bye'.

'That was your friend – Detective Chief Inspector Wilde...
says he wants a word. He's on his way round.'

'What does the bastard want?'

'Fuck knows,' said Charlie. 'get those biscuits back over
here.'

I pushed the packet back across the table. 'Did Wilde hint at
what was on his mind?'

'Relax, if he was going to nick you he wouldn't have
phoned first. You shouldn't take all this crap so seriously. Try
getting some more sleep. You've got big dark rings around yer
peepers.'

Twenty minutes later there was a knock on the door and
Charlie ushered in a peely-wally looking Wilde. 'Ye look like
death warmed up,' said Charlie, 'want tea?'

I looked at him the same way a mongoose does a snake.

'No, I'll come straight to the point.' Wilde sneezed
violently, wiped his nose and carried on. 'You'll probably both
know by now that it was Tijuana McCormack's headless
remains we fished out the Clyde.' We nodded. 'His head
eventually turned up to confirm matters.'

'So?' I said

'So Sunny Jim, that means your partner in crime is probably
alive.'

'And?'

'And,' said Wilde, 'there was an arson attack on his office
last night.'

'No kidding,' said Charlie. 'Who would want tae do a thing
like that?'

I just stared at Wilde waiting for the strike.

'Oh, maybe somebody like a well known Glasgow
criminal,' said Wilde pulling out his well used handkerchief, 'I

hear he got made a fool of yesterday. Somebody conned him with a lump of gold painted lead. You know, you...' He paused, waiting for the sneeze, then spluttered into the hanky. He peered at the mucus for a second, then stuffed it back into his coat pocket.

'You were saying?' I said.

'I was saying,' continued Wilde, 'that you shouldn't get smart. There were reports of a gunshot being heard from within this criminal's pub. Two men were seen running from it – one fits your description.'

'Got a body to go with this incident?' I said.

'No, you were lucky, you survived,' said Wilde. 'Mind if I sit down? This cold is knackering me.' He drew back a chair from the table. 'I think I will take a cup of tea after all.'

I looked over at Charlie but he wasn't going to make it, so I sighed, went to stub out my cig in the sink and put the kettle on.

'There's also a rumour going around the town, said Wilde helping himself to a biscuit, 'that there's a stash of Nazi loot somewhere.'

'We've heard the stories,' said Charlie, 'they've been on the go for years.'

I said nothing, knowing fine that Wilde had ransacked Van Luben's house and the Bumble's office.

'There could be some truth in the matter,' said Wilde.

The kettle boiled and I filled the teapot. Wilde put another biscuit to the sword. Nobody spoke. 'All right, all right, you know that I know there's slightly more to the Nazi angle.' He drew out a brown envelope from his inside coat pocket, unfolded a letter and held it up.

'What's this?' I said placing the teapot on the table, 'Your resignation?'

Wilde gave me a sarcastic smile. 'No, it's from a detective agency in Zurich confirming, from Swiss wartime records that gold was withdrawn in early May 1941 by...well never mind who by, but the gold could well be here in Glasgow.'

Neither Charlie nor I responded.

Wilde reached for a mug. 'Look, you pair of eejits, do ye no want a piece of the pie? There's a reward for its return and if a few bars of gold were to be lost, well...'

'Mind who you're calling eejits,' said Charlie, this is my house and you're here at my invitation.'

'Well if yer interested, let me know pronto... since my last unofficial partner seems to have done a runner.'

'You mean the Bumble?' I said.

Wilde nodded. 'If you see him tell him I want a word. Don't suppose you know where he is?' Again he was met with silence.

'Okay, okay, I get the message. By the way, I've just come from his sister's place.' Wilde lifted the empty biscuit wrapper. 'Got any more?'

'Get on with it,' I teased out a fresh cigarette from the packet.'

'Tony McCaffrey's body has been released for disposal. Thought you might like to know. Anyway must be on my way. You make a good cup of tea by the way. I'll show myself out. Mind and don't take to long to make your minds up... ye know where to reach me.' He got up to go turned and made his fingers like a gun, pointed them at me and moved his thumb down simulating the hammer action. 'I would get some life insurance if I were you – if you intend to stay in Glasgow that is. So long cowboy.'

I watched him slither off. We heard the front door opening. Wilde shouted back through, 'Oh, and by the way, the old guy you hauled out of the fire says thanks, you might even get a commendation for bravery.'

Charlie opened a cupboard and handed down more chocolate digestives and picked up his newspaper. 'Want your horoscope for the coming week from Mystic Morag? Gemini isn't it? May 21-June 20.'

I nodded.

'If you dwell on the array of minor disasters you've been contending with over the recent weeks you could work yourself into a real state.' Charlie lowered the paper. 'See, just what I've been telling you, anyway it also says that you shouldn't bother about recent disputes and that it will all turn to your advantage. Not even a mention of Uranus being fucked over by friends.'

'Very droll,' I said. 'We'll have to find the Bumble.'

Chapter 15

The next few days were relatively quiet – thankfully. Nobody tried to kill me, and with a watchful eye over my shoulder I managed to visit a few old acquaintances. I even found time to go and visit my father. He hadn't moved in almost twenty years. I'm not sure he would have approved of the pink carnations I laid beside his grey granite headstone. I contemplated the memories I had of him until a sleet shower came on. Sheltering under a Yew tree I lit a cigarette with cold fingers and glanced at the rows of headstones and the dark laden sky.

I thought of Tony, he was due for cremation. Officially there was nothing to prove his death was murder. It was classed as misadventure. As I said a guy on the end of a rope in a gay man's flat, with a selection of sex mags around, doesn't attract a lot of police interest. He made it into *The Daily Record* and the *Evening Times*, but with no details beyond his age and where he had been found. Shoving my hands into my side pockets of my coat I made my way back to the living.

I shaved my tired face under the glare of the overhead lamp slowly drawing the disposable razor over several days of growth. The blade tugged at the whiskers, I smiled widely drawing the skin back to help the process. At moments I caught my father staring back at me – the same calculating hazel eyes, the same look of discontent, the same dark hair cut with a number three setting on the electric clippers once a month. I nicked the side of my nostril and cursed then dabbed it with a towel and wiped my face dry.

It had just gone one thirty when there was a loud rap on the front door.

'Come oan. Up and at em,' said Charlie not waiting for an invite to come in. 'We've got a funeral tae go to.'

Christ, it's Wyatt fucking Earp, I thought as I looked him up and down in his all black funereal outfit. He took a gold pocket watch from his waistcoat and checked the time. It was attached to an Albert chain from which a purple gemstone hung.

'Or more correctly,' he added, 'a date at the Cremmie down at Masonhill.'

My mind tried to do a quick calculation on the location. 'Where?'

'It's down at Ayr, if ye'd remembered.'

'Ayr?'

'Aye, Ayr... you know, land of Rabbie Burns, down the coast.'

'Ayr?' I said again.

'It's where the McCaffreys came from before they moved up tae Glasgow.'

I lit a cig and stepped out into the cold light of day.

'You've been watching *Gunfight at the OK Corral* again,' I said.

'Nothing wrong with a bit of a tradition on a solemn occasion.' Charlie flicked an invisible speck from his coat.

I had to take my hat off to him. He looked every inch the chief mourner even though he wasn't. I got into the Capri. The driver's door opened and as Charlie climbed in, I detected a slight whiff of mothballs from his suit but thought better of saying anything.

'Want to borrow a black tie?' he said.

'Never wore one for him in life so why bother in death?'

'Okay, okay, just thought I'd ask.'

The Capri fired up and we headed out of Glasgow, southwest over the Fenwick moor towards Ayr. It was bleak and misty and snow lay in patches. This was the historic land of the Covenanters, the fundamentalists of the Presbyterian faith. It was also the land that time forgot.

'Believe you get judged then?' I said, stretching back and enjoying the blast of heat from the blower. 'Fires of hell and all that?'

Charlie dropped the Capri down a gear overtaking some slower moving traffic. 'Philosophical today are we?'

'Maybe,' I said and turned the radio on. Cliff Richard warbled on about mistletoe and wine.

'We've got a tail,' said Charlie, 'Black Audi back there... been with us since we left Glasgow.'

I looked in the door mirror. 'Sure?'

'Watch this.'

Charlie floored the accelerator and the nose of the Capri lifted. I watched the black Audi do likewise.

'Who do you reckon it is, then?' I said.

Charlie picked up a toffee from a paper poke between the seats and began to chew. 'Does'nae really matter does it? All roads lead to Masonhill.'

We found the crematorium without too much bother and parked up. The black Audi did likewise a short distance away.

'We'll wait here until the hearse arrives,' said Charlie. 'Want a coffee?'

'Toffee?'

'No, *coffee*. You've gone hard of hearing these days. Should get your lugs syringed out.'

'It's not my lugs. I was just wondering where you were going to get coffee round here, unless the Crematorium has installed a vending machine.'

Charlie thought that was worth suggesting to the local council, along with a CD selection of all time funeral greats. He leaned over the back of the seat, rummaged in a dark blue Rangers sports bag and brought out a red tartan flask.

'Be prepared,' he said, pouring coffee into a plastic cup. He handed it to me, and it was welcome. As I sipped on it I couldn't help but look towards the misted windows of the Audi. I wondered who its occupants might be. I also wondered if Kev Barr would show up with a posse as things had gone unnaturally quiet on that front.

Charlie slipped a cassette into the stereo. A piano tinkled and Elvis began to sing *How Great thou Art*. I raised my eyebrows.

'I like a sense of occasion,' he said. 'Who better than the King?' He relaxed back in his seat chewing away. The King said it all *"Oh Lord my God, when I consider all the worlds thy hands have made..."*

The hearse arrived. I glanced at the pine coffin covered in flowers that spelled TONY and clocked the immediate family in a black stretch Volvo.

'We'll wait until they all file in,' said Charlie, unwrapping another toffee.

We watched various people, including the Marmalade Cat, decant from the limousine and make their way inside.

'They reckon,' I said, 'that most killers like to show up at the murder victim's send off. That's why police film the event.'

'If that's the case where are they?' said Charlie, 'He died by his own hand – come on, let's go and pay our respects.'

Sleety rain pelted us as we made a dash for the Chapel. We found an empty pew near the back and surveyed the gathering of mourners. I began to put names to faces. The Marmalade Cat sat in the front row, beside her the guy and girl I had disturbed at the Bumble's party. On the end sat a grey-haired woman in a brown fur coat. She was the only one who looked genuinely upset. Behind them there was an array of old dearies that could have been relatives, but maybe they were just bored souls who enjoyed a day out from the local retirement home. A few hard nuts with solemn faces ambled in and sat a few rows in front. I nudged Charlie. 'Know any of them?'

'No.'

I gave Charlie another nudge. 'Think anybody is going to say anything?'

'Like what? That masturbation can be hazardous to your health? Especially if you place a rope around yer neck and suspend yerself from a door?'

'You know damn fine it was Kev Barr and the Russian who did it.'

'You've only Kev's word that they killed him, I keep telling you that. You know how twisted he can be. He claims every violent crime in Glasgow to bolster his reputation, whether he had anything to do with it or not. He gets hassled by the cops, he tells them he's outraged – who was defaming him? Present the evidence or piss off. He's a game player – albeit a dangerous one. Short of a written confession with reliable witnesses what have you got?'

The pallbearers brought in their charge. There was a rustling of coats and quiet coughs as everybody stood and watched the coffin being placed on the altar platform. The attendants covered it with the flowers from the hearse, bowed and then retired out of sight – no doubt for a quick fag before the next job. From a side door at the front of the chapel, a guy in a dog collar appeared and assumed his position in the pulpit. 'Let us lift our voices to God and sing Psalm 23, The Lord is my Shepherd.'

Charlie's voice boomed out in a flat bass. *'My soul he doth restore again; and me to walk doth make, within the paths of righteousness.'*

I closed the hymnbook as voices faded with the final line of the last verse.

'Please be seated,' the man of God requested. 'We come here today to pay our respects to Anthony McCaffrey, a much respected young man who cared for friends and family alike...'

'Have we got the right funeral?' I whispered to Charlie. Christ, I thought, somebody must have given him a sizable backhander to lavish such praise on a low-life like Tony. Then just as it had begun, it was over. Nobody gave a eulogy. The Chaplin asked us all to be understanding at a time of grief for the family and to be upstanding for the benediction.

'Lord receive this soul of our dearly departed brother into your keeping, in the name of the Father, the Son and the Holy Ghost, amen.' And with that, Tony, in his pine overcoat, slid into the furnace while the curtains swished back into place and piped organ music played a sympathetic air by Bach. Some punters blew into their hankies while others rubbed their eyes.

'I'm an atheist at heart so this is all bollocks to me,' said a familiar voice from behind.

We both turned to see Detective Chief Inspector Wilde with a large guy who had a mouth like a hen's arse.

'This is the Lord's House,' said Charlie, breaking into the ecumenical dispute. 'Show some respect. We'll shoot the breeze in due course but not until we've paid our respects tae Tony's family, so button yer lip.'

Wilde hesitated for a second then shuffled out with his sidekick.

'That's the trouble,' said Charlie, 'dignity tends to go out of the window these days.'

We all filed out and shook hands with the bereaved at the entrance to the Chapel. As I took Linda McCaffrey's hand, I muttered, 'Sorry about the other night.'

She held onto my hand a little longer than was polite. 'Thank you for being here,' she said. 'There's a drink at the Seaview Hotel in the town square. You're welcome to come.'

'Thanks,' I said and moved on. There's something about funerals that sharpens your sense of mortality. I lit a cigarette.

Wilde caught my eye. 'What's Burke and Hare doing here?' I said and snapped my lighter shut.

'Thought the Bumble might show,' said Wilde, having a look round. 'See you've been getting acquainted with the grieving mother as well.'

I looked over at Linda who was speaking to one of the old codgers, took a draw on my fag and returned my attention to Wilde. 'So?' I asked dryly.

'Nothing,' said Wilde and sneezed. He wiped his nose with the back of his hand. His colleague proffered a packet of tissues.

'Don't suppose,' said Wilde, 'you've talked to that fat bastard yet?'

'No' I said, 'we'll let him know you were asking for him when we do – that okay?'

'He has until Christmas Eve and then like Jacob Marley's ghost, I'm going to rattle some chains at him.'

'C'mon,' said Charlie, heading for the Capri, 'It's bloody brass monkeys standing out here. Lets get down to the Hotel for a few jars.'

At the Seaview Hotel we were met by a black bear that had been caught and stuffed by Jack the Ripper, judging by the amount of stitches it had running up its front. The mourners had gathered in a mirrored room, which tried to emulate a downmarket Versailles. Waiting staff smiled politely offering drinks from their trays. People mingled with an assortment of refreshments in hand trying to act cheerful and recount witty tales about the deceased. I had none to tell.

I felt a touch on the shoulder. 'Sorry for the intrusion,' said the Marmalade Cat, 'I was wondering if I might have a word?'

'Don't mind me,' said Wilde, with amusement on his face. 'I feel the need for something warming.' He headed for the bar with his assistant. Charlie gave his condolences and went in search of a sandwich tray and another whisky.

'I'm sorry to interrupt,' Linda paused and I could see she'd registered my apprehension at her approach. 'I'll come to the point. We both know Tony was difficult and not above the law when it came to making a few quid.' I felt there was something else, something more coming. 'He couldn't have died the way he did. I just don't believe it.'

'Why don't you go talk to the police?' I opened my packet of Marlboros and offered her one.

'The police? Don't make me laugh. Do you really think they properly investigated his death? Look around you. Do you see any honest cops here? No, to them he was scum... somebody that gave them the odd bit of information.'

'Why are you telling me this?'

Her eyes looked directly into mine again.

'I thought you might like to work for me... sort of make up for the mistrust that seems to have built up between us.'

'Why don't you ask Davie when he surfaces? Or Charlie over there?'

'Please,' she said, 'I want discretion, not the full highlights of Tony's death doing rounds of the Glasgow pubs.'

I glanced over at Charlie who was in conversation with Wilde.

'I'll be honest,' I said striking my lighter, 'there could be any amount of people out there with grudges against Tony, just as I mentioned before... one in particular with enough motive to maybe murder him... but maybe it was just an accident after all.'

'How about you investigate a bit further,' she said with coldness in her eyes, 'and I don't wander over there and tell Chief Inspector Wilde that it wasn't Davie that found Tony but you – and who knows, maybe it was *you* that strung him up.'

'He was long dead by the time I arrived.'

'The police don't know that – do they?'

Kitty had claws. I eyed her with suspicion rather than hostility. 'What are you after?'

'Just a little of the truth. Was there anything that seemed out of place when you found him?'

'Apart from the rope around his neck?' A thought hit me as I looked at her – there was something out of place – the

Crucifix. Okay, I know there are those who commit crime and think they're going to be absolved because they bite chunks out of the alter rail or make a donation to the Church, but I hadn't Tony down as that type – nor as a born again. Maybe the Crucifix had been a simple bit of fashion, nothing more because the Marmalade Cat was now wearing an identical cross.

I took a slow draw on my fag and said, 'I thought Catholics bury their dead?'

'Eh?' said the Marmalade Cat.

'Tony – I presumed it would be a Roman Catholic service and burial afterwards.'

'What are you talking about? Tony was never near a church in his life. Frank, his father, was practically ex-communicated after he physically threw the parish priest out the house.'

'Why?'

'Is this really relevant right now?'

'I guess not,' I said, watching her subconsciously touch the Crucifix. 'I also guess you got Tony's only worldly goods.'

Linda drew her hand sharply away from her neck and looked towards Wilde. Instead of telling her to go and spin on it, I found myself agreeing to her request. 'Okay, I'll ask around but don't expect immediate results.'

She opened the gold clasp of her black designer handbag and handed me an envelope. 'There's two hundred in there, make up for the sex we didn't have.' The Marmalade Cat knew how to recover her position.

'I'll give you a call,' I said and pocketed the cash. It was the first time I'd been rewarded for disappointing a woman.

'Fine.' She touched the back of my hand and strolled off towards the other mourners. I noticed Charlie looking over and stroking his moustache. He looked like Joe Stalin before a show trial where some poor bastard ended up in a gulag for the rest of their natural. I went across to join him.

'Linda seems interested in you all of a sudden. After a bit of Yuletide log was she?'

I ignored him. The lassie behind the bar smiled and asked what I would like to drink.

'Whisky please.' I studied the carved stone face of a man on the wall of the bar.' Who's the fella?' I asked.

'It's the Green Man,' she said.

Probably the lager, I thought, and slugged back the contents of my glass.

Chapter 16

I've heard it said that people sometimes feel as though a higher force guided them to where they are. Right now I was contemplating a list of names and their connection to Van Luben, Tony McCaffrey and Rudolf Hess – all deceased. I trusted in the great Architect, closed my eyes and stabbed the pen into a page on my notebook – God had chosen the Chinaman. I poured a coffee and rang him. He still had sleep in his voice.

'Been entertaining?' I said.

'Oh, it's yerself... yes, as a matter of fact I...'

'Listen Reuben I haven't time.'

'That's what they all say.' He chuckled.

'Listen to me, how would you like an exclusive?'

'Fire away I'm all ears.

I related the whole works to him.

'Love it!' he said. 'Greed, intrigue, murder, mystery, and men in uniforms!'

'Cut the camp act for a second. It could also be dangerous, with nutters like Kev Barr and unknown parties out there.'

'That's what good journalism is all about,' he said.

'Okay, but in return I need someone to identify a possible Nazi.'

'Don't tell me you think Rudolf Hess is alive and well and living in Glasgow?'

'No,' I said and took a sip of coffee, 'he'd be receiving telegrams from the Queen congratulating him on reaching his hundredth birthday and beyond.'

'Someone to ID a Nazi, eh?' He only needed to think about it for a second or two. 'Aaron Schoenberg.'

'Sounds promising,' I said.

'He's a solicitor, runs a firm by the name of Beaumont and McGinty. Grew up in the Warsaw Ghetto... survived Auschwitz. He runs a legal practice out at Possilpark these days.'

'Possilpark?' I said incredulously.

'Yeah as the saying goes where there's muck there's brass. The lower orders always need the services of a good defence lawyer and a decent suit. He has, shall we say, contacts, with various Israeli organisations – so I'm told. He'll be able to check out the punters in the photograph with Van Luben.'

'Okay, I'll go see him,' I said, 'and I'll be back in touch, but mind and say nothing for the moment, even if it's just to stay healthy.'

'Mum's the word,' said the Chinaman, and a Merry Christmas when it comes.'

I said goodbye and topped up my coffee.

Charlie lowered the morning paper. 'Well?'

'Looks like we're taking a trip out to Possilpark.'

He looked at me as though I gone completely mad.

'It's fucking Apache country out there. It's the sort of place where you lock your car doors when you're still inside the vehicle. Ah hope yer no expecting me to take the Capri out there. Christ man! It would be up on bricks the first traffic light we stopped at.'

'Fair enough, I get the picture.' I bit into a piece of buttered toast slathered in marmalade.

'Anyway,' said Charlie, 'I've got a bit of work on this morning. Couple of statements to take. Mind though, if you need me, give me a bell on the mobile.'

'Okay, and you won't forget we need to find the Bumble later on?'

'Dinnae worry, he won't be far. I've got a location for his latest girlfriend.'

I found Beaumont and McGinty's address in the phonebook and caught a bus to Possilpark. It was a place where an ill wind always blew and where a cat with a tail was called *Lucky*. I lit a cigarette and strolled past an arcade of graffiti-covered shops with metal shutters that looked ready for a siege. Locals trekked back and forth wearing the obligatory fashion of shell-suits, baseball caps and Burberry. Most had dogs as accessories, the choice being pit bulls or greyhound-type mutts with spindly legs.

The solicitor's office was a grey grill-covered cement blockhouse sitting on derelict waste ground. It wouldn't have looked out of place on the Western Front. I stood at the entrance to Beaumont and McGinty and studied a couple of signs on the inside of the door. A formal one indicated that they offered Legal Aid. Another, handwritten on a sheet of paper, stated that 'No dogs, unaccompanied children, drinks, drugs or foodstuff' were to be brought into the premises. I knocked the glass door and when the release mechanism buzzed, I pushed it open and found myself in a waiting room.

The air was thick with cigarette smoke as punters sat around the walls on stained cloth-covered bench seats that spewed foam stuffing from where they had been slashed. They resembled a pirate crew of Blackbeard's that had been press-ganged the night before and thrown into a ship's hold. There were guys with razor scars, unwashed spotty juveniles, and women with black eyes. I strolled up to the receptionist who sat behind a reinforced Perspex screen with a porthole that said: *Speak Here.* I spoke.

'I'd like to see Mr Schoenberg.'

A wee tough-looking woman in her mid fifties with white roots showing through her chestnut hair raised her head by a fraction, adjusted her red-framed designer glasses and said, 'Got an appointment?'

'No,' I said, 'but it's urgent that I talk to him.'

'It always is,' she said. 'When's yer court appearance due?'

'I'm not here for anything like that,' I said. 'Tell Mr Schoenberg that Rudolf Hess wants to see him.'

I figured it would buy me entry. She didn't bat an eyelid at the name. I'm sure if the real Rudolf Hess stepped into Beaumont & McGinty's office he would have fitted right in with the crowd waiting for advice. Maybe they would have done him a better service than he got at his trial at Nuremberg.

'He's with a client,' the receptionist said. 'You'll have to wait till he's free.'

I took a seat. The old white-haired guy on my left immediately began to tell me his reason for coming to see Mr Schoenberg.

'Fell doon a hole,' he said. He told me his son had videoed the hole, as proof. Whether he'd remained in it for the filming was unclear, but anyway he wanted his 'compensation'.

On my right sat Mr Stale. Stale clothes, stale tobacco, stale body odour and stale boozy breath. All he needed to complete the scene was a cloud of flies hovering above his head. I fished out my packet of cigs, sparked one up and added to the fug.

Twenty minutes later a burly guy with a confident smile and a fine collection of sovereign rings on each hand strolled out from the consulting room and left the premises. He had obviously been promised a get out of jail free card. The receptionist disappeared through the back. Several minutes later the door to the side of the corridor opened and a small portly dark haired man, about mid sixties stepped out. He resembled Toad of Toad Hall in a pinstripe suit.

'Mr Hess?' he said without hesitation.

I got up and followed him. He ushered me into an office that stank of dead rodents and cigars. Umpteen air fresheners had been placed around the room in a vain attempt to mask the odour.

'Have a seat,' he said and sat down behind a functional metal desk. 'What can I do for you Mr Hess?'

I was tempted to say to him, 'Please, call me Rudolf,' but I didn't. 'It's about handling stolen goods,' I said and smiled.

He was cagey but played along. 'Have you been charged? Do you have a court date?'

I laughed as though I had just been released from an institution that very morning.

'It can be a serious matter,' he said, unwrapping the cellophane from a packet of King Edward cigars.

'Aye, I suppose it can. Yeah there were some charges.' I brought out my cigs.

'Do you wish to apply for Legal Aid, Mr Hess?'

I laughed again and he looked even more bewildered.

'Sorry Mr Schoenberg, maybe I should explain. Reuben McKenzie gave me your name. The charges for handling stolen goods were levelled against a slick bunch of criminals called Nazis.'

Toad of Toad Hall's eyes widened.

'Nazis?' he said.

'Yes, one in particular. Rudolf Hess... I presume you've heard the story of him flying here and bailing out south of the city?'

He nodded and said, 'I don't know what this has to do with me.'

I held the flame of my lighter under my cigarette, inhaled and looked directly at him and allowed tumbleweed to blow through for a second or so. 'I came here because Reuben McKenzie told me you were in a concentration camp or something as a kid and have contacts.' I snapped the lid of my lighter shut.

There was a silence. He studied me with calculation then pruned the end of his cigar with a trimmer.

'Carry on,' he said, 'I see you've done your homework.'

'See, it's like this, I believe Rudolf Hess brought gold with him, and was aided by people we would now call sleepers. One in particular was a well known car dealer in Glasgow, Peter Van Luben.'

'I've heard of him,' he said poking a vent into his cigar with a match.

'Van Luben wasn't the only one, though. I believe there were others. I handed a photocopy of the old newspaper article across.

He reached for the pair of gilt framed glasses suspended on a chain around his neck, placed them on the bridge of his nose and studied the group. 'I recognise some of these faces from around Glasgow.'

'Could you make enquiries?' I said.

He removed his glasses. 'Why should I do that?'

'Because if I find some Nazi gold, I might return it to its legitimate owners.' I paused and added. 'Or their descendants – and of course a finder's fee would be welcome.'

He struck the match, lit his cigar and sat back. 'How do I know this isn't some hoax thought up by you for whatever reason. Or by one of my disgruntled clients Mr..'

'You don't,' I said, 'but trust me.'

'Do you have a contact number?'

'No,' I replied, 'I'll call you. I need to know everything you can find out.'

He nodded. 'Give me a few days. You understand that I will have to check this out with my contacts.'

'Just one more thing, did you know that gent there?'

He donned his glasses again and I indicated Frank McCaffrey with my index finger.

'Frank McCaffrey – yes, I represented him a few times... it was a number of years ago. Left a pretty young wife if I remember.'

I smiled and offered him my hand. He hesitated then shook it. 'I'll be in touch,' I said and closed the door behind me. That force that people believe in had worked. Schoenberg was as bent as they came and no amount of air fresheners was going to disguise it. The Chinaman had also been the only name in my notebook.

The reception area had filled up with several more dodgy punters having bad face days. They all seemed to be protesting their innocence to anyone who would listen. I zipped up my jacket and opened the main door. Breathing some fresh air, I strolled off in search of a phone box.

Chapter 17

The only thing that had bothered me about Possilpark had been trying to find a phone box that actually worked – or one that hadn't been used as a urinal or had dog shit dobbed on the receiver. Yes, I was coming round to the idea of having a mobile phone.

I eventually managed to call Charlie from a pay phone inside a general store run by Mr Ali. 'The Bumble,' I said, 'what address have you got for his squeeze?' I wrote it down. 'Kersland Street, right see you there about 2 o' clock.'

I sat on the top deck of the bus back into town and watched an empty blue and gold Tenant's super lager can rolling back and forth on the floor in between surveying my fellow passengers; some were plastered despite it just gone lunch time, some were high, others just dejected. Their toughness ranged like a steak from rare to rock hard. A few teenagers sat at the very back exchanging their latest experiences of having spent time in a holding tank courtesy of the Glasgow Polis. One declared that he was too smart to have been apprehended with any gear on him, another that he was probably going to get community service since he had no previous convictions, while the third musketeer was hacked off that some acquaintance in the cell refused to share the plastic wrapped drugs stuffed up his arse.

'Man!' declared the youth, 'Ye could hear the fucker crinkle every time he moved.'

The sky had become black as I got to the tenements of Kersland Street. Icy rain came on as I hung about waiting for Charlie. Handling the Bumble myself wouldn't be a problem – in fact I was positively looking forward to it. But things recently were quiet, too quiet.

I just didn't want to get up there to find a surprise Christmas party going on – with Kev and Tango in festive paper hats wanting to do the Hokey Cokey while singing *You put your left boot in and kick it all about* followed by the right boot and Tango barking approval at such merrymaking.

I stood in the doorway of the next block, cupped my hands and blew into them for a bit of warmth. I went to light a cig but my Zippo had run dry. Cursing I looked up and down the street for a punter to stop and ask for a light but there was nobody about. There was a store across the other side of the road so I went over and bought a can of lighter fluid and a box of matches making a mental note to refill my lighter later. Outside a couple of teenage Asian girls kicked a football off the wall in a style that would have put any Scottish team to shame. I heard Charlie's Capri before I saw it; the rumbling V6 had a distinctive sound. He drew along side us, parked, got out and locked his treasured classic.

'This it?' I asked, looking up at the building.

'Aye.'

The main entrance wasn't locked so we headed up the stairs. We stopped on the third floor outside a door with *MacDonald* on a red tartan nameplate.

'Think he's in there?' I said.

'I've run down his other bolt holes and nothing.'

'What do you reckon?' I said. 'Shall we knock?'

'What was that?'

A low moan emanated from within. Charlie rapped the door. We waited a minute or so and tried again.

The noise stopped.

'I don't like it,' I said.

'Stand back,' said Charlie. He took a few backward paces then charged the door. As he reached it, it swung open. There was nothing he could do, as the momentum he'd generated carried him past the shocked figure of Priscilla in a scarlet silk dressing gown. She didn't offer any challenge to the sudden intrusion and flattened herself against the wall. There was a loud crash as eighteen-odd stone collided with an old hallstand. From somewhere in the flat I heard the Bumble shout. 'Whit the fuck is going on?'

Stepping inside I quietly closed the door. 'Where is the fat bastard?' I said, glowering at Priscilla.

Stunned, she simply pointed to a door on the left. Charlie was effing and blinding as he picked himself up and sought to vent his wrath on someone for his misfortune. Luckily the Bumble was available. Taking Priscilla by the arm I pushed her through the door that she had indicated, while Charlie bemoaned the damage to his attire and pride.

We surveyed the purple walls and the king size bed with its leopard skin headboard and bed cover. A cat o' nine tails hung from the bedpost.

'Christ! Talk about coitus interruptus!' said the Bumble.

He sat up in bed resplendent in a white singlet that needed the Daz doorstep challenge. I guess we were it. I threw a

Marlboro to him then lit my own. He stuck the cig in his mouth. 'Got a light then?' he said, unabashed by our entrance.

'Sure,' I said and strolled over to the bed. I took out the can of lighter fluid and sprinkled it over the bedclothes that covered his fat carcass.

'Hey! Whit the fuck are you doing?' He attempted to get out of the bed I pushed him back and struck a match.

'Move, and your chestnuts get toasted,' I said. 'You almost got me and your brother killed you fucker! Switching the gold bars and loading the gun with blanks – that your idea of a laugh?'

'You're still here,' he said, 'aren't you?'

'Yeah only just. Your brother was crapping it when Kev Barr took the gun off me and started to play Russian Roulette with him. And I was the finale in the show, he pulled the trigger with my guts as the target.'

'Good job they were blanks then. You got Jim out?'

I nodded. 'Aye. You don't give a monkey's, do you?'

'I told you, you would do it, I've got faith in your abilities – now if I had sent you along with live ammunition we wouldn't be having this conversation. Would we? My eejit of a brother is free and we've still got a block of gold worth a few quid – I'd call that a result.'

'You're fucking priceless,' I said.

'Tell me, did Kev find it funny?'

'Yeah, how did you guess?'

'Just call it intuition.'

'Never mind Kev Barr finding it funny, I'm now the laughing stock of the city, Christ even Wilde knows about it.'

'You'll get over it.'

'We want to know the score,' I said, 'and not just the half time one that you've been feeding us so far.'

'Hey doll, said the Bumble, 'going to put the kettle on while I catch up with the lads here?'

Priscilla glared at Charlie and myself and made an exit. I struck a match and held it over the bedclothes.

'There's nae need for this you know,' said the Bumble.

'My thoughts exactly Davie, but I felt you deserved a little of your own medicine. The icing on the cake was my arse almost getting fried down at your office,' I blew out the flame of the match before it reached my finger tips and made to strike another.

'What dae ye mean... fried at my office?'

'Davie, don't insult my intelligence. I went looking for you after your sister told me you had phoned her.'

'When?'

'The day you done your disappearance act, late on.'

He pondered and said, 'Aye, I think I did call her.'

'She thought you were down your office.'

'Doing what?'

'Writing your last will and testament, given the amount of folk wanting to chat to you.'

'Look, lads... okay I switched the ingot, but would you have walked in there if I told you to take along a painted lump of lead? And why would I attempt to kill you?'

'As I see it Davie, you couldn't lose, even if I never came back.'

'Just torch the bastard,' said Charlie, 'he'll live long enough for us tae get the truth out of him.' He meant it.

I struck the match for good measure.

'Okay, okay, I'm getting to the point.' The Bumble's arse was squirming. 'As you know, they found Van Luben's widow deid and Wilde investigated it... then I had a prowl out there as well...' He paused and looked up. There was more. Apart from the gold bar I found a stash of banknotes he'd overlooked.'

'How much?' I asked.

He hesitated.

The second match burned out. I let it drop to the carpet. I pulled another one from the box. 'Three strikes and you're out,' I said.

'Hundred odd thousand,' he said with a sigh.

I let out a whistle and turned to look at Charlie, whose jaw had slackened somewhat.

'Does Wilde know?' I asked.

'No, he and the rest of Glasgow think there's a stash of Nazi gold somewhere. I had to tell them something to keep them off the scent... and the ingot was ideal especially with the rumours about Van Luben.' The Bumble smiled, genuinely pleased with himself.

Brilliant. Gold fever was sweeping Glasgow bringing out every fucking ned, nutter and corrupt cop in the city, thanks to the Bumble.

'You realise, Davie, that there's a posse of fucking psychopaths out there in search of Eldorado.

'There's *definitely* more than one ingot,' said the Bumble. 'Mind, I told you about Tony taking the documents and showing them to that guy who runs a militaria shop?'

I nodded and flicked my ash into a pewter ashtray that featured a naked couple making the beast with two backs.

'Well, that's when the trouble started. As you know, Kev Barr showed up, but there was also this other punter who turned up at my office demanding the Nazi documents, saying he would'nae leave without them and I thought...'

I interrupted him. 'What was this character like?'

'About mid-seventies, well dressed... oh and he wore a macabre bloody silver ring... ye know like bikers wear... a skull design.'

I frowned over at Charlie who simply shrugged.

'Got any proof of what you're saying?' I said.

'Aye,' said the Bumble, 'if ye go intae the wardrobe over there it's in the suit jacket.'

'What am I looking for?' I said pushing through black and pink basques, a PVC raincoat, corsets and various lingerie garments that were designed for more intimate moments.

'It's in one of the side pockets there, a black card embossed with silver lettering.'

I rummaged some more, ignoring the packet of fruit flavoured condoms, and found the card and held it up. It was black with silver embossed letters. It had four capitals that spelled H.I.A.G. and a telephone/fax number at the bottom right hand side.

'H.I.A.G.' I read out.

'Haig?' said Charlie. 'Was the guy a whisky rep then?'

The Bumble and I exchanged looks.

'I take it he wasn't a whisky rep,' I said.

'No,' said the Bumble, 'I did'nae get that impression.'

'So how did you leave things with the man from H.I.A.G?' I asked.

'Turned him down. Come on. With so many punters sniffing around these documents they had tae be something worth having.'

'Did this guy leave a name?' I said.

'No, I told him tae go bile his heid.'

'So do you reckon he was after the gold or the money?'

'I reckon the money had nothing to do with the Nazis,' said the Bumble. 'The cash was nothing more than undeclared takings from Van Luben's businesses... more than likely.

I crushed out my cig in the ashtray and extracted another one from the packet. 'You sure of that?'

'Aye, most business guys have a roll of cash under the floorboards, just a matter of knowing where to look.'

I was sure he was holding out on us. I lit the cigarette and dropped the lighted match. The bedclothes instantly took on a bluish hue as they ignited. It only took a split second for the Bumble to register the fact. Legging it out of his pit, he threw the covers onto the carpet and stamped them out.

'You fucking bastard! That could have done me some permanent damage!'

'I don't like being kept in the dark... or being made a mug of,' I said, 'and you conveniently left out the part about the money... or were we not included in the divi?'

As the Bumble stood there I couldn't help but stare in disbelief at his pasty hairy legs and his white boxer shorts with pink cupids on them.

He looked down at them. 'What? I was trying to spice up our love life... give us a break!'

'We can now tell DCI Wilde that you are alive and well. He's been round to see us with an offer.'

'Been asking for me has he?'

'Aye, for a while he had you down as a headless corpse.' I told him about Tijuana McCormack.

'The bastard must have dipped my pocket at the station when I caught the underground. I wondered where my wallet went.'

'Tea or coffee?' shouted Priscilla from the kitchen.

'Tea,' replied Charlie, 'and some biscuits sweetheart.'

'You owe me,' I said and threw the Bumble's trousers to him. 'Big time. You also missed your nephew's funeral. Get dressed and we'll have a chat in the parlour.'

Charlie and I wandered through to find Priscilla in the kitchen.

'In there,' she said and jerked her thumb towards a door. The room was festooned in red and silver Christmas hangings. Cards were strung out along the walls and a decorated Christmas tree sat by the window. A few moments later Priscilla followed us into the lounge with mugs and biscuits on a tray.

'Nae chocolate ones?' enquired Charlie while casting an expert eye over the selection on offer.

'Yer bloody lucky I'm giving you anything at all,' said Priscilla and sat beside me on the red leather settee. She flicked her dyed black hair from her face and crossed her legs. A fluffy black mule balanced on her right foot. 'Got a spare fag?' she said, forcing a smile.

I handed her my packet.

'Ta.' She lit up with a cheap yellow plastic lighter.

'Nice *pied-a-terre* you've got here,' I said noticing a tattoo of a tongue at the top of her bare thigh. 'Nice original features.'

'Drop dead,' she replied, and pulled the side of her dressing gown over her leg.

Charlie reached for a mug and lifted a biscuit.

'Hmm, custard creams, nae bad I suppose.'

The Bumble ambled in zipping up his flies. 'Thanks doll.' He picked up my cigarettes and helped himself to a smoke. Sitting down, he took a draw, let out a stream of smoke and held his arms open like a father greeting a long lost child. 'What can I say? Sorry, I didn't think things were going to turn out the way they did.'

'And when,' I said, 'were you going to surface?'

'Soon,' he said, rolling his hand with the cigarette in it like a royal wave.

'What? When a few more bodies turned up? How about you start treating us like equal partners or I pick up the phone and tell Kev Barr and Wilde where you are.'

'C'mon, c'mon,' said the Bumble and spooned several sugars into a mug of tea. 'There's no need for that. I'll cut you in for an even share of the gold.'

'Just the gold?'

'The money has nothing to do with you!' said Priscilla, with a look that Bette Davis would have envied.

'Look,' I said, 'considering the amount of shit that's come my way courtesy of lover boy here, an even split of everything is the least he could do to amend the wrongs visited upon my ass. Besides, if he doesn't cough up I'm going to make sure that a rottweiler, by the name of Tango, gets to wear his bollocks for earrings at the Hole in The Wall public house Christmas party! Dig?'

The Bumble sighed. 'The cash is in a suitcase on top of the wardrobe in the bedroom.'

Chapter 18

I brought the tan suitcase through to the lounge, flicked back the chrome locks and whistled.

'So, what were you planning on? Sending us a postcard from Hawaii?'

'Naw, naw,' said the Bumble, lying like a cheap rug.

'We don't have tae give you lot anything,' stated Priscilla. 'Finders keepers.'

'Sweetheart,' said Charlie, 'you won't make it out the city.'

'Hard man eh?'

'Fact,' said Charlie, munching another biscuit.

'Lets keep a lid on this,' I said and closed the case. 'We'll talk about a divi up later. Tony had a reasonable send off by the way.'

'Oh,' said the Bumble.

'Aye, oh,' I said. 'Could you not have put an appearance in?'

'Funerals can spell trouble. I'm sure Tony would have understood.'

'Talking of the deceased, he's not really related to you, is he?'

'No, I guess not,' said the Bumble, 'but Linda doted on him, they were close.'

'Did she ask you to find him?'

For a second he hesitated. 'She was concerned for him, taking off the way he did... I never told her about the Nazi stuff he took. I simply offered to find him.'

'And then I came along.'

The Bumble sighed. 'And then you came along.'

'Okay... the gold,' I said and tapped the column of ash from my cigarette into the cut glass ashtray. 'What makes you so damn sure that there's more out there?'

'Just a hunch and yon geezer with the ring.'

'Was he in that photograph?' I said.

'What photograph?'

'The one in the newspaper that was under you lino in your office.'

'Whit? What are you talking about.'

'The old newspaper you stashed away. It showed Van Luben and his mates having a celebration – on Hitler's birthday.'

'You been on a bit of Rastafarian bliss?'

'No.' I brought out the article from my inside pocket and unfolded it.

The Bumble studied it. 'Never seen it before in my life.'

I pointed to Frank McCaffrey. 'There's one of your in-laws with Van Luben.'

He re-examined it. 'Christ, so there is,' he said as though it was the most natural thing in the world. 'I never realised Frank knew him. Fancy that.'

'Yeah,' I said taking a sip of tea, 'fancy that. Does that tell you anything?'

'Like what? That he was a crook? Frank McCaffrey knew every major criminal in Glasgow. He was part of a family circle in a manner of speaking.'

'And what did your sister know about his dealings?'

'Not much, I would imagine. Linda was too happy with the life-style he gave her to ask awkward questions.'

'But with Frank gone, who runs his empire?'

'I don't know.' the Bumble shrugged. 'Most of his businesses were sold off I guess.'

'Enough for Linda to be comfortable for the rest of her natural then?'

'I guess,' said the Bumble 'where are you going with this?'

'Nowhere yet.' I helped myself to a custard cream. 'Anyway have you got the original letter allowing withdrawal from this Swiss bank allegedly used by Hess?'

The Bumble nodded. 'It's through in the bedroom, I'll go and get it.'

He reappeared waving it around like Neville Chamberlain on his return from Munich.

'I don't suppose you've got a fax machine here?' I asked and drained the contents of my mug. The Bumble shook his head.

'Right, then I'm away out,' I said, 'but I need a couple of items from you... namely the letter here and your mobile phone. Oh and you'd better show me how it works and give me its number.'

The Bumble looked at Charlie and then me.

'Don't worry, Charlie will stay to make sure you don't vanish with the cash and that unwelcome visitors don't pillage the place.'

The Bumble shook his head. 'Nah, it was'nae that. You must be the last guy in Britain not tae have a mobile phone, that's all.'

'Yeah, yeah, I've been meaning to get one. Anyway I'm off to send this, so you'll all behave yourselves for Charlie won't you!'

'How do we know that ye'll come back?' said the Bumble.

'A hundred thousand reasons.'

'Get me a packet of fags when yer out,' said Priscilla. 'Super Kings if they have them.'

'Got the cash?'

I received a mock smile. 'Do I look as though I've got money on my person?'

I found a shop a short distance away on Great Western Road that looked as though it might have what I needed. It was one of those multi-service places that offered everything from dry cleaning to colonic irrigation. I was in luck. They had a photocopier. I made additional copies of the document then phoned Aaron Schoenberg. He didn't have any information as yet but he was expecting something soon. I told him I was about to fax him a letter and that it was possibly related to the gold angle and could he also check it out for authenticity. I asked him if he knew what H.I.A.G stood for but he hadn't heard of it. I told him how to reach us and hung up.

I examined the phone number on the black and silver card and dialled the man from H.I.A.G. – it went straight to answerphone. 'If you're interested in German artefacts, call,' I said and read out the Bumble's mobile number.

I handed a tenner to the Asian shopkeeper along with one of the copies of the letter for him to fax. A couple of minutes later he handed us confirmation that it had gone through.

'Anything else,' he enquired.

'Twenty Super Kings, twenty Marlboros and a packet of milk chocolate digestives.'

I headed back. Charlie opened the door. 'Here,' I said and handed him the biscuits, 'I could murder another cup of tea.'

The Bumble and Priscilla were watching some inane cookery show about stuffing your turkey. The Bumble turned and asked if I got sorted out and I nodded in return. Taking out his mobile phone and the letter I placed them on the coffee table then threw my jacket over the back of the settee.

'So what's happening?' he asked.

'We wait,' I said.

'For what?' he enquired.

'For the mountain to come to Mohammed.' I told him what I had done and asked if the tea in the pot was fresh.

'Did ye get me my fags?' enquired Priscilla.

I threw them across to her, wondering what the Bumble saw in her beyond a shag.

'I would'nae mind something tae eat,' said Charlie.

'Right Davie,' I said, 'get your wallet out and we'll order a take-away.'

'It was stolen, mind?'

'What are we having anyhow?' said Charlie, 'Pizza or fish and chips?'

'Pizza?' said the Bumble in a mortified tone. 'I want a Ruby Murray.'

'I canny stand curries,' said Charlie.

'That's typical of you McLeod, you never could hold down anything spicy.' The Bumble opened my fresh packet of cigs.

'Listen,' said Charlie, 'your idea of holding down something spicy is having a grope at a waitress in a Tandoori restaurant. I'm happy with the Pizza.'

The Bumble's mobile phone rang. We all looked at each other in silence. Picking it up I quietly said, 'Hello?'

It was Aaron Schoenberg.

Everybody was eager to know who it was.

'Is it that bastard from HIAG's?' asked the Bumble. I waved to him to keep his voice down while I wrote some details.

'Right,' I said, 'be in touch. Bye.'

'Well?' said the Bumble.

I took a cigarette from the packet and lit up. I looked at the Bumble and then the note pad.

'Do you know what H.I.A.G. represents?' I said letting out a long stream of smoke. The Bumble shook his head.

'Want to know?' I raised my eyebrows.

'Get on with it,' said the Bumble.

'*Hilfsgemeinschaft auf Gegenseitigkeit der Soldaten Der Ehemaligen Waffen-SS,*' I said in my best German.

Charlie gave me a look of 'is that a fact?'

'It's a mutual aid society,' I said, 'for former soldiers of the Waffen SS, Davie. That's why the punter that came to see you was wearing a death's head ring. It looks like Hess took some of their pension fund investments.' I took another deep draw on my cig. There was silence for a moment.

'Can we get back tae deciding whit tae eat,' said Priscilla, 'cause ma stomach thinks ma throat's been cut.'

Wishful thinking I thought.

'Well I'm no having a bloody curry and that's final!' said Charlie.

'Right,' said the Bumble, 'we'll order you a European dish, that okay?'

'Aye, but mind not a drop of fucking curry near it!'

Jesus H. Christ!' I muttered under my breath.

The Bumble went over to a drawer in the sideboard and brought out a take-away menu for the Star of Bengal

Restaurant. Twenty minutes later we had finally reached a conclusion on the voting for the food and called it in. Then the Bumble's mobile phone rang again.

'Yes,' I said and paused as I listened to the other party who had an exaggerated German accent. He was cagey and not into talking over the phone. He wanted to meet. I suggested the café bar upstairs at Central Station at midday tomorrow.

'How will I know you?' he asked.

'I'll be whistling *Tomorrow Belongs to Me*. I'm sure you're familiar with the Hitler Youth anthem.' I hung up.

The Bumble looked at me again. 'I'm not even going to ask,' he said, 'but are ye sure ye know what you're doing?'

'Aye,' said the Queen of the Dead. 'Ye could be selling us all down the river.' Again that was wishful thinking.

Half an hour later the buzzer went. We all just looked at each other then it went again.

'I'll go,' said Charlie and a few moments later he shouted through that it was the take-away.

Minutes later we were all tucking in to a selection of offerings from the east. Even Charlie was a happy chapatti with his steak and chips, while the Bumble sweated like a navvy over his curry.

Eventually, there were sighs of satisfaction.

'Could go another cup of tea doll,' said the Bumble.

'Then get off yer arse and make it,' she said reaching for her cigarettes.

I relaxed back into the settee and glanced at the Advent calendar. I reached over and picked open the final door. There before me was an angel with three wise men bearing frankincense, myrrh and gold.

Chapter 19

The Bumble sat back sweating, licked his lips and picked a strand of curried beef from his teeth. He would have probably taken them out and sooked them if he wasn't in company. He mopped the remnants of his curry sauce with a piece of nan bread. Drips fell on his trousers.

'You know, that was bloody good!' he said, wiping the perspiration from his forehead with a hanky. The Bumble looked at the lust of his life. 'Go on doll, make us another pot of tea.'

She got up under protest and wandered off to the kitchen. His mobile phone rang. The Bumble leaned forward, picked it up and said, 'Hello?' in a confident manner.

Charlie and myself watched him as his expression of contentment changed.

'Oh, it's you... aye, my phone's been switched off. Whit do you mean you're out of money? And you want me to bail you out?' The Bumble covered the mouthpiece of the phone with his hand. 'It's my brother Jim, he's out of money in some crummy hotel not far from here.'

Christ I thought, I'd almost forgotten about him. 'Tell him to get a taxi,' I said, 'and come over, we'll pay for it.'

'Whit!' protested the Bumble.

'Well where else is he going to go? He must have been trying to get in touch for days.'

Like worried parents we sat and waited for him to arrive. Twenty minutes later there was a polite tapping on the front door. Nobody moved.

'Christ,' said the Bumble, 'I suppose I'll have to let him in.'

'He's your relative,' said Priscilla and started to refresh the bright red varnish on her fingernails.

There were quiet 'hellos' from the hallway and in stepped Jim Cowan.

He sported several days growth. I stood up. 'Hello Jim, good to see you. What took you so long to get in touch with Fats here?'

'Been trying the office phone for ages and leaving messages on the mobile.'

I gave the Bumble a stare.

'Whit? I've been busy,' he protested, 'and besides the office phone is out of action – isn't it?'

Jim Cowan nodded to Charlie and then Priscilla.

'Sit down,' said the Bumble.

'Tea Jim?' I said and offered a cigarette.

'I'm no making it again,' stated Priscilla without glancing up from her repaint.

'Charlie and I will make it,' I said. 'Jim and Davie can reminisce about old times.'

I couldn't hear a lot of chatter as I washed out some cups and made a fresh brew while Charlie chewed on a toffee and eavesdropped by the kitchen door. Maybe like most dysfunctional families, it was one of those unnatural moments when you're expected to have fondness for each other when in reality, disdain bobbed just below the surface.

'Here we go,' I said and placed the tray on the coffee table. 'Help yourselves.'

'Jim's thinking of going away,' said the Bumble, slurping his tea. There was a large chunk of hope in his voice.

'really?' I said trying to be actually concerned.

'Aye,' said Jim, 'all the carry on with... well you know. My nerves are at breaking point. I don't fancy ending up in that pub cellar again getting a gun put to my head... or a police cell for that matter. I know I should have gone to the cops and talked to them.'

'Bit late,' said the Bumble and extracted a cigarette from the packet in front of him. 'They'll only think you had a reason to run.'

I was going to mention Tony's funeral and then thought better of it.

'Managed to get a passport,' said Jim nibbling a chocolate digestive like a rabbit that had found a prime piece of lettuce. 'Always carried my birth certificate on me.'

'Least you've *got* a birth certificate,' said Charlie, 'unlike your brother.'

'Whit are you inferring?' said the Bumble. 'That I'm a bastard?'

'If the coat fits,' said Charlie and topped up his mug with a splash more of milk from the carton.

'Listen,' said the Bumble, 'I'll have you know I was thinking of him all the time...'

'Might be a good idea,' I said cutting in before a major argument erupted, 'for Jim to get away.'

Jim Cowan coughed, 'I was hoping...'

'That Davie could lend you some cash,' I interjected, 'shouldn't be a problem to a man of his means.'

'Now wait a wee minute...' said the Bumble. 'If you think...'

'Otherwise,' said Jim quietly, 'I might have to go to the authorities after all... no money... no home... and...' He nibbled some more.

'Okay, okay,' said the Bumble, 'I get the picture, if I don't give you some money you'll make things awkward.'

I had underestimated Jim Cowan. He was as capable as the rest of his siblings.

'I was hoping I could rest up here tonight,' he said, 'freshen up a bit before I head off.'

Priscilla looked none too happy.

'We'll stay as well,' I said with a wink towards the Bumble, 'just to make sure that arrangements remain as they are. Let's see if there are any holiday films on the telly eh? Or watch a video... providing your selection isn't all of the adult type.'

'I'll sort your cash out tomorrow,' said the Bumble grudgingly.

'Thanks Davie,' said Jim, 'I knew you would come through for me... what's family for after all?'

'Do me a favour,' said the Bumble and picked up the TV Times Christmas edition beside his chair, 'don't come back looking for more.'

Priscilla switched on the telly. We settled on a special edition of a game show where celebrities spun a wheel for money. The proceeds went to charity, naturally. The remains of the day were based round tea, food and moderate quantities of alcohol.

'Lets have a game of cards,' suggested the Bumble, 'be like old times.'

'For real money?' said Charlie. 'I don't believe in gambling as you know. I never wanted anything to do with your card school, even Ernie Bilko would have got fleeced.'

'Why don't we try strip poker?' said Priscilla.

The Bumble froze.

'Relax,' she said 'I was only kidding.'

'How about we use the cash next door?' said the Bumble.

It was Priscilla's turn to freeze. She glared at him and motioned with her eyes towards the Bumble's brother.

'Aye, well,' said the Bumble, 'perhaps not. We could watch a movie.'

We settled on a western – *The Good, The Bad and The Ugly* seemed appropriate. Priscilla distributed blankets and retired to the bedroom.

By the end of the film Charlie was asleep. Jim Cowan was slumped over the arm of the settee and showed no sign of movement.

The Bumble yawned. 'Well, time to hit the hay.' He studied his brother for a moment. 'He was always my Ma's favourite.' He carefully covered him with a green travelling rug. 'I'll gae him a few quid... you don't think he had anything to do with Tony's death?'

I shook my head. 'No I don't.'

'Night then,' said the Bumble and switched the telly off.

I draped a wool blanket round myself and tried to get comfortable in the chair listening to the noise of the city for a while. Out the back, a couple of cats must have been having a rumble as high pitched screeching echoed around the enclosed back green. Then it went quiet until the Bumble and Priscilla decided to have a rumble as well. She went into orgasmic shouts then a final screech of fulfilment. Charlie was sawing wood. Wearily, I glanced over at the Bumble's brother who appeared to be definitely out for the count. I guess it was life Jim, even if it wasn't as I knew it.

I awoke to a dawn chorus. 'For fuck's sake!' shouted the Bumble.

I shielded my eyes from the glare of the overhead light in the lounge. 'What are you yelling for? Christ what time is it?'

'Never mind the fucking time!' The Bumble held the suitcase that had contained the money. He opened it and held it in front of me, all I could see was the beige chequered lining. 'Empty! Fucking empty!' he roared. 'That bastard of a brother of mine. Bastard!' He threw it towards the vacated settee. 'Wee bastard!'

Wearily, I sat up, rummaged the contents of the coffee table and found my fags under an empty chocolate box. I drew out a couple and handed one to the Bumble. 'Calm down,' I said, 'before you have a stroke.' I offered him a light.

He paused for a draw on his cig, retied the cord on his leopard skin dressing gown and continued his rant. 'Left a fucking goodbye note, says he actually only wanted to use the suitcase ...he's only at the airport buying a stand by flight to God knows where for Christmas.' The Bumble paused for breath and took another draw.

The lounge door opened, 'Whit the fuck is going on?' asked Priscilla, a cigarette between her lips. 'Whit are you yelling about?'

The Bumble sighed. 'He's taken the fucking money... says he's sorry but he couldn't help it.'

Priscilla did a quick head count. 'Are you having a laugh?'

The Bumble braced himself for the onslaught of Hell. Her mascara encrusted eyes widened. 'You useless piece of shit! I told you we should have put the money under the mattress and slept on it! But no, nobody here was going tae nick it! Too busy getting yer end away last night to care! Jesus fucking Christ! I had us spending Christmas in Tenerife or somewhere! Now it's just you, me and this dump.' She paused for a quick flick of her fag, 'A hundred thousand quid! In that wee shite's hands tae squander!' She puffed on the cigarette some more and then ground it into the ashtray, probably wishing it were Jim Cowan's face.

'I didn't invite him here doll,' pleaded the Bumble, for the defence.

Priscilla stared at me. 'How was I to know?' I said.

She turned and left the room with a slam of the door.

Charlie yawned and stretched his arms. He unwrapped a toffee and flicked the silver foil wrapper into the air. I watched it disappear past the Bumble's head. 'Want to go out to the airport?' he said. 'See if we can find him? If not maybe you could get yourself a one way ticket away from that nippy sweetie you call a girlfriend.'

The Bumble sighed. 'Och, she'll come round and besides its ten o' clock, he could have left here hours ago. He's probably at twenty thousand feet fluttering his eyelashes at an air steward... fuck! We'd better see if the gold ingot is still next-door, it was in Priscilla's handbag. Christ! Maybe he fancied that as well!' Despair was written over his face as he promptly went to search for it.'

'It's still here,' he shouted through, 'best if Priscilla looks after it, eh?'

I glanced at Charlie with raised eyebrows. The Bumble wandered back in, sat down and lit another cigarette.

'Got a hacksaw?' said Charlie.

'Whit do you want a hacksaw for?' said the Bumble.

'Tae cut the gold bar into three pieces, I want my share now.'

'And whit about me?' said Priscilla from the doorway.

'You're with him,' stated Charlie, 'and you weren't keen to give us a share of the money.'

Before a ramification kicked off, I flicked the switch for the lights on the Christmas tree. 'Lets just leave the gold as it is,' I said, 'and have some breakfast. Look on the bright side we've still got something of value and the chance of some reward money.

'Mr fucking optimistic can make some tea,' said Priscilla still simmering.

'Reward money?' said the Bumble.

'Wilde says he'll cut us in for a share of it.'

'Wilde can get stuffed,' said the Bumble and continued to curse his brother.

I helped to cook a fry up of bacon and eggs during the seasonal truce that followed.

'I'm off home,' said Charlie dabbing his moustache. He downed his coffee. 'You coming?'

I didn't see any point in hanging around with the two lovebirds. 'Aye, may as well.' I eased myself out of the armchair. Lifting the Bumble's mobile from the coffee table I gave it a check over. 'Don't mind if I borrow your phone, Davie, just in case our interested parties have a change of plan or something? This is the only number they've got.' I didn't wait for an answer and pocketed it.

'Listen,' said the Bumble, 'just don't pull any fast ones, if ye come up with anything, cause I've still got the original document that accessed the gold in Switzerland.'

I buttoned my coat and looked down at him. He was in the process of pouring himself and Priscilla a whisky.

'Dinnae get any fancy ideas neither,' he said and added soda water to the drinks. 'We're all in this deal together.'

'Yeah, yeah,' I said. 'I'll give you a bell after I meet the H.I.A.G. guy.'

Charlie didn't say much on the way back over. I opened the glove compartment and took several swigs from the half bottle. I offered Charlie some but he declined.

'Are you bothered about the money?' he asked.

'Not really,' I said, 'Jim Cowan can build himself a new life. Maybe it's the Christmas gift he's been waiting for.'

'Yer getting pretty philosophical these days... want some company for meeting this guy?'

'Nah, you're okay. I figure he wants to talk and besides that's the reason I chose Central Station... too many punters about for anything serious to happen.'

'Ye reckon?' said Charlie, accelerating the Capri with a graceful change of gears as the red light at a junction changed.

'I reckon,' I said screwing the top back on the whisky bottle.

Chapter 20

I looked at my watch – it had just gone eleven. Charlie dropped me off and I headed into the city centre for a stroll before my meeting at high noon. The underground was packed to the gunnels as the Christmas lemmings crammed in eager to spend, spend, spend, on something to please or appease.

It was Christmas Eve. I walked along remembering people I'd met in the city centre shops, bars and restaurants from years ago. Euphoria at being taken as a child to the Clyde Model Dockyard down Buchanan Street Arcade to be treated to a precision made model – this was a city of engineering after all. My father worked in the shipyards, my grandfathers worked in the shipyards, my great grandfathers worked in the shipyards. I was Clyde built.

I bought a coffee in one of those global establishments that are run by bean counters, a deluxe latte thing where it's three quarters froth and costs you several quid and the staff have the effrontery to place a begging bowl in front of the till for your change. I declined the loyalty card and the pre-pay option.

It was still only half eleven but I thought I might as well head over to Central Station and be early for the meeting. Maybe the Hun would appreciate me being on time. I wondered what you would buy a Nazi for Christmas – a touring map of Poland? Or maybe the Rough Guide to Russia? On the other hand, maybe he'd prefer a CD: *The Führer's 20 Greatest Rants – Live on Stage at Zeppelin Stadium, Nuremberg.*

There seemed no end of people as I pushed my way along Gordon Street and crossed over to the main arched entrance for Central Station. Taxis picked up and dropped off. Travellers sought directions both in and out of the city. People with more important things on their minds brushed past a Big Issue seller in a wheelchair peddling his magazine.

I glanced at the large railway clock that hung in the centre of the Victorian industrial cathedral, 11:45. The coffee and the cold were beginning to have an adverse effect on my bladder so I paid my twenty pence into the barrier at the station toilets, pushed against the turnstile and selected a cubicle to have a pish in peace. I bolted the door behind me and with great satisfaction relieved my bladder of its contents. Then, just as I was about to give the matter in hand a good shake, I heard this male voice.

'Oh go oan, ye might like it!'

Must be an old hand with a young apprentice, I thought. The next cubical definitely had more than one occupant. I heard lowered voices and the rustling of clothes. Zipping up, I coughed loudly and flushed the bog. Maybe I'm a little old fashioned about sex, but I prefer pleasanter locations than somewhere with the smell of urine and disinfectant hanging in the air. As I slid back the bolt on my cubicle door, I heard a grunt of satisfaction. Someone was coming early for Christmas. Washing my hands, I headed back up the stairs to the mildly pleasanter environs of the concourse.

The upstairs cafe overlooking the station was busy but I managed to find a seat at a window that gave an excellent view of the punters below. I bought another coffee and looked at the station clock. Ten to twelve. Down below I noticed Transport Police going back and forward with a brown and white Spaniel sniffer dog. Some teenagers got huckled by the fast food outlets. They had to empty their pockets while the police mutt sat looking pleased with itself. Personally, I'd have made it eat whatever was found for infringing civil liberties. Then I'd have thrown it over into the cubicle with the two cottagers in it. Dugs! I lit a cig and resumed my people-watching.

'Good morning, this seat is free?'

Turning round I saw a guy in his late sixties-early seventies in a long slate blue leather coat with matching belt. His narrow skull was capped with thinning white hair. He had a well-trimmed beard and gold-rimmed glasses framed his eyes. A thin red scar ran across his cheek. I watched him as he took off his black leather gloves.

'May I?' he said.

'Be my guest.' At least he's polite, I thought.

He took off the coat, draped it over a chair, and then sat down. I took a draw on my cig and gave him another look over.

'Cigarette?' I gestured the open packet towards him.

'No, thanks,' he replied and began to drink his coffee.

His accent had changed since yesterday.

'Do you want a look at the papers?' I said and reached for my inside pocket. He looked surprised and said he had seen them already, so I left them where they were. 'So how much are they worth?' I said, rolling my cigarette between my fingers and looking directly at him.

'Worth?' he said.

'Yeah, how much?' I took a draw. He looked decidedly nervous.

'Depends' He swallowed a large mouthful of his coffee.

'On what?' I asked and stubbed out my cig.

'Content usually,' he said, draining his cup quickly. 'Excuse me, but I've a train to catch.' With that he got up and put on his leather coat.

'You don't want the papers?' I said puzzled as to why he was leaving.

He reached inside his coat, brought out a copy of the Daily Express and placed it on the table.

'Here,' he said, 'you have this, since your need appears greater than mine.'

It suddenly dawned on me: I had the wrong punter. I shouted thanks as he made a swift exit.

I checked the station clock again. It was five past – my real date was late. Then I saw a wee bloke with grey hair and a large bristly moustache standing looking around. I watched him carefully as he headed towards my table.

'Ze chair is free?' he asked, his keen blue eyes monitoring me.

I nodded but I wasn't about to repeat my mistake. 'Just one thing,' I said. 'Can I see your ring?'

He smiled and revealed a Death's Head silver band on his left hand.

'Sit down, Pops,' I said, 'and let's get down to business.'

'Goot.' He brought out an old metal cigarette case, opened it and offered me a cigarette. 'Turkish, very, very goot.'

'I have not smoked anyzing else since ze Vor, but let us not talk about such matters.'

167

I took one of his cigs and lit it. He turned and said: 'Ze documents, you have zem?' I snapped my Zippo shut.

His accent was worse than his Turkish cigs. It was like something out of a British war movie where all the Huns speak comic book English.

I nodded. 'So, Pops, you were a member of the SS then? Bet you saw some action?'

'Ah ze Vor. Ya, I was on ze eastern front... a terrible place... but come let us not talk about such conflicts.'

I studied his trench coat – it was threadbare around the cuffs. I noted the nicotine stains on the fingers of his right hand. I reckoned the nearest he had been to the Eastern front was a trip to Whitley Bay.

'So how much are you getting paid for this performance?' I said. The man's face changed and he narrowed his eyes.

'I don't know vat you mean.'

'Listen, Pops, the last time I heard an accent like that was on the sit-com, *Allo Allo*.'

He let out a thin stream of smoke, then looked down at the table. 'All right pal,' he said, 'Ah guess German accents are'nae ma best. Ah needed the money for Christmas cos I did'nae get a part in the panto this year, up at the Kings Theatre.'

'What part did you go for? I said. 'The horse's arse?'

'Okay son, take the piss but ah used tae be a good character actor. Been in *High Road* and *Taggart*, so I have.'

'I've news for you,' I said, 'you're about to make another appearance in a cheap drama – as the body. Who sent you?'

'Ah cannae tell you son. He would kill me for real.' He looked nervously out of the window. 'Look son, ah'm sorry. Ah only did it for the money.' He got up and hurried out.

There wasn't any point in going after him, so I let him go. I watched him scuttle across the concourse then I froze at what I saw next. It was Kev Barr. The elderly thespian got grabbed by the collar and pointed up in my direction. Christ! I thought, that must have been one of Kev's numbers on the H.I.A.G. card – it was a complete set up. He'd used his brain.

Kev Barr shoved the old guy to one side and, along with Tango and his strong-arm sidekick, began to cut a path through the punters, like Charlton Heston parting the Red Sea. It was time for brawn.

I was in deep shit.

There seemed to be no escape for me as they headed towards the cafe but God saw all and smote the mighty fat bastard. Well no' exactly God – but a Spaniel attached to a copper's wrist. It was practically breakdancing in front of Kev. The performing mutt must've detected he was carrying some gear. Kev looked up at the cafe menacingly as he was apprehended. His minder tried to disappear into the crowd but got his collar felt by another large cop. Kev was obviously professing his innocence loudly. Then more police arrived as a small crowd gathered. Tango didn't bark approvingly though as he was muzzled.

Kev was now being escorted away to the Police office up by platform 13. Unlucky for some. He gave me a well-practiced death stare, so I gave him a smile and then a middle finger.

There was a God after all.

Chapter 21

I sighed with relief and wandered over to the counter and bought another coffee. Settling back into my seat I reached to my inside pocket for the mobile phone. I hoped Kev would be having Christmas lunch in the Bar-L – Barlinnie prison. For a second I thought about Tango and wished him well. I dialled a number from my notebook.

It rang out and I was just about to hang up when the party I was after answered. 'Hello?' a female voice said.

'It's me,' I said to the Marmalade Cat. 'Thought you might like an update for your money – or you can have a refund and a roll in the hay instead.'

'Talk,' she said.

'I don't know if it's any consolation, but Kev Barr has been arrested. Might be away for a few years.' There was silence for a second or two.

'And that's it?'

'Pretty much,' I replied and lit a cigarette. 'Oh, almost forgot to mention – the other party, your brother Jim. He stopped over at Davie's last night. Disappeared early this morning and took a hundred grand with him.'

'What?'

I explained about the cash. 'Seems he's also left the country.'

Her thoughts focused on a word that conveyed sexual intercourse and an alternative description of the vagina. Christmas can be such an upsetting time of year, especially for families. I got the reaction I had expected from her. 'Hope you haven't bought him a Christmas present.'

'Cut the sarcasm,' she said. 'I didn't employ you for opinion, just fact.'

'Well, if we're on facts most people die at the hands of somebody they know,' I continued, 'often a family member, so everybody keeps telling me – but I don't have your brother in the frame, he's an opportunist, just like Tony was. And also for the record I don't think Kev Barr killed him.'

'What are you saying then?'

'Call it heartburn from too much coffee,' I said taking a sip, 'but no, the flat was too unmolested. Kev and his companion don't buy into good housekeeping when they want to find something.'

She changed the subject. 'And Davie, where exactly is he?'

I told her. She deserved to know.

I flicked ash from my cig into the saucer. 'Before you get out your electric carving knife,' I said, 'do you still want me to work for you?' I tried a shot in the dark. 'I would almost guarantee that the cash belonged to you.'

She repeated the sexual reference and hung up. Nothing like a woman ripped off to bring the wrath to the fore. The station announcer uttered some intelligible message for passengers.

I'd thought I'd shake the pear tree and see if any more partridges were up there. I scanned my notebook and punched in another number. Yet again a female voice answered – it was

Aaron Schoenberg's receptionist. 'Tell Mr Schoenberg Rudolf Hess needs to speak to him – urgently.' I gave her my number, took a final draw of my cig and crushed it out.

I watched the flotsam and jetsam of humans below for a moment or two, moved at times by humans actually pleased to see each other. Then the mobile rang. It was Aaron Schoenberg.

I told him my end of things first and he said he wasn't surprised but to be careful because the H.I.A.G. organisation was for real and they were capable of their own intelligence gathering – even in Glasgow. He had managed to identify the last man standing in the photograph. He was, according to Social Security records, Alfred Kaminski, aged 88, living at 110 Keir Hardie Street, Dumbarton.

Not much of a place to end your days I thought.

'There's not many who can hide these days,' said Schoenberg. 'Everybody leaves a trail and when you look...well I won't bore you with the details.'

'I presume with a name like that he's a Pole? What would he be doing associating with a Nazi like Van Luben?'

'The Germans had volunteers from all over Europe my friend, even amongst the Polish, many were forced to fight for Germany. Poland also had areas that included German Poles – hence the alleged reason for war by Hitler. They were the reason Germany invaded Poland in 1939. They wanted their people to be part of the greater Germany.'

I thanked him for the history lesson. 'And I suppose you want me to pay him a visit?'

Schoenberg laughed. 'Naturally. You are better placed to do that,' he said. 'My presence might compromise things.'

'You think he knows something about the gold?'

'Maybe... and your action would not go unrewarded if you find anything... also should something happened to him... well...'

'Look,' I said 'I'm not an assassin of old men.'

'No,' said Schoenberg, 'but he was.'

I didn't say anything for a few seconds and then mentioned Wilde. He laughed again. 'The world is full of corrupt policemen,' he said. It's an occupational hazard, especially for me.'

'Okay,' I said getting out my cigs. 'I'll pay the guy a visit and let you know.' I paused to light up. 'Oh and a Merry Christmas.'

'I'm Jewish,' he said.

'I know,' I replied. The line went dead. I got myself a bacon roll and a fresh coffee. Down below, in the centre of the Station concourse, the Salvation Army band struck up *Good King Wenceslas.* I thought over what Schoenberg had said and wondered if pursuing ghosts was the ideal way to spend Christmas Eve but I suppose Dickens had the copyright on that angle.

I phoned the Bumble and told him I had some possible good news while he had some bad on the way – was he still interested?'

'What the fuck did you go and tell Linda about the money for? Jesus H. Christ!'

'She was my client and the hundred thousand was hers.

'Your what?'

'You heard.'

'Since when do you work for her? I bloody pay you!'

'Yeah, yeah, keep your corset on. You never found that money at Van Luben's house, did you?' There was a silent

173

pause. 'It was your sister's cash. Her stepson Tony stole it –
didn't he?'

'Possibly,' said the Bumble.

'And you convinced him to leave the money with you for
safe keeping the night he allegedly ripped off the documents.'

'Perhaps.'

'What did you do? Show him the gold bar the same as me?
Cut him in for a share if he showed good faith by taking the
documents to that militaria guy to test the water? And your
sister wouldn't think you'd rip her off – would she?'

'Alright, alright. He showed up with the suitcase. At first I
didn't know what was in it. Then he told me about the money
that Linda had tucked away under the floorboards. The
remainder, according to Tony, of his father's undeclared
earnings. He figured he was entitled to it as his son.'

'As simple as that,' I said.

'I had to give Tony some collateral,' said the Bumble. 'To
convince him to leave the cash for safe-keeping. I showed him
the German documents and asked him to get them checked out.
Then I don't hear anything from him.'

'Look,' I said, 'I think your sister is involved with Tony's
death. She had the motive. I think he contacted her and she
paid him a visit in Edinburgh and killed him.'

'Have you been on the sauce? He was her son for Christ
sake!'

'Stepson,' I corrected, 'and money, gold, mullah, cash – lots
of it can change a person's personality – if she had one to
begin with.'

'You saying she went through tae Edinburgh, lassoed him,
and strangled him to death?'

'With a cry of *Yee hah!*' I said, taking a sip of lukewarm coffee that had been made with burnt milk.

'You're sick.'

'That may be true,' I said, 'but I might be able to prove what I'm saying.'

'Okay Sherlock what's the plan?'

'If she shows up at your end, fob her off. Tell her you didn't realise the cash was hers. Tell her how inept you were over losing it – she'll probably believe you.'

'You looking tae get your lights punched out?'

'Tell her you're onto another big deal, something better than her lost fortune, but that you're waiting on more information.'

'And then what?'

'And then nothing. Get rid of her and I'll be round later to identify your body.'

'Ha, bloody ha.'

'Phone Charlie,' I said, 'and tell him to come over.'

The Salvation Army band was still playing as I said my farewells to the Bumble.

On my way out of the station I dropped a few quid into the open instrument case that doubled as a collection box for God's musicians. It was the least I could do to thank him for still having the ability to walk.

An hour later I was back at Priscilla's flat on Kersland Street.

'Man!' said the Bumble opening the flat door, 'you know how tae land folk in shite!'

'Make a change from me being in it,' I said and brushed past him.

'Christ! I thought I'd never get rid of Linda. Her and Priscilla were screaming and shouting at each other – she's vowed revenge on us.'

'Who? Priscilla or your sister?'

'Dinnae get smart.'

'Well Davie, what did you expect trying to rip off your own sister – sympathy?'

'All right, all right.'

'Did you do as I said and tell her about the possibility of other treasures?'

'Aye, she was spearing the arse out of me for details.'

'But you kept her guessing?'

'What do you think? Course I did. You really think she killed Tony?'

'We'll know soon enough.' I gave him the finer details of Kev's arrest. 'So where's Charlie?'

'He'll be round shortly.'

I yawned then lit a cig. 'Where's the Queen of the Dead?'

'Will ye weesht! And don't let Priscilla hear you call her that. Lucky she's away to her office party.'

'Want a coffee?' I said.

'Aye, go on. You know where the kitchen is, I'm watching a *Star Trek* movie, it's a good one.'

Somebody rapped the main door with a firm conviction.

'Going tae get that,' the Bumble shouted, 'it'll probably be Charlie.'

It was.

'Kettle's just boiled,' I said, 'you want a cup of something.'

He nodded.

Five minutes later we convened our meeting.

'Well? What's so bloody urgent?' said Charlie. 'Another family member rob you?'

The Bumble forced a smile and nodded in my direction. 'He's got the address of the last guy standing in the Van Luben photograph.'

I related my conversation with Schoenberg. 'Our destination for tonight is Dumbarton. Where we're hopefully going tae meet Alfred Kaminski.'

'Who the fuck his he?' said the Bumble.

'The last surviving person that knew Van Luben well enough to know what happened to the gold... if Hess brought it here,' I said. 'He lives at Keir Hardie Street, in Dumbarton to be precise.

'Whereabouts is Keir Hardie Street?' asked Charlie unwrapping a toffee.

'Bottom of the Bonhill estate,' I replied.

'Christ!' the Bumble said, 'that's fucking Geronimo country, even I know that... weans, dugs, drug dealers. It's Ned Central.'

'So we've tae pay this old guy a visit,' said Charlie. And do what?'

The Bumble turned round, 'Aye, whit exactly are we going tae do at Keir Hardie street? Threaten tae take his pan drop mints if he dis'nae know anything about the gold? Come oan I know solicitors of old... they can be dodgy bastards, friends to the criminal fraternity. Schoenberg will have an angle tae this.'

'Oh and you're snow white?' I said, 'after the stunts you've pulled recently?'

'No,' the Bumble said, 'but I'm wary. How did he find the guy after all these years?'

'He has connections... look what have we got to lose?' I sat back in the armchair.

The Bumble reached for my packet of cigs, 'So we just go up tae his door and tell him we're the three wise men looking for a few bars of gold tae take with us on a divine mission?'

'Okay,' I said, 'I haven't got that part figured out... but he's the last surviving link in the chain... according to Schoenberg... for finding the gold. What have we to lose? Maybe we could strike a deal with the old bloke. Take the pass book for the Swiss account, offer him a share or something.'

'Whit if he's nae in when we get there?' said the Bumble with a slurp from his mug. 'He could be down the boozer, at the Bingo or singing *Silent Night* at the Church.' He flicked the ash from his cig.

'Are we going down tae Dumbarton or not?' said Charlie.

'Aye, we're going,' I said.

The Bumble looked round and said, 'As soon as this movie is finished.'

'Whose motor will we take then?' enquired the Bumble.

'We'll take the Capri, I said, 'it'll blend better in the local environment.'

'You trying tae say I drive a low life motor?' Charlie's tone was indignant.

'No,' I said, 'you drive a piece of automotive history.' I returned my gaze to the telly as Captain Kirk asked Ohura if her circuits were working.

'Why not go tomorrow?' said the Bumble. 'Would'nae take long in the morning and he's bound to be in.'

'No,' I said, 'I don't want anyone stealing a march on us.' We sat back and watched whales being transported to the 25th Century.

A short while later there was the sound of a key turning a lock. The front door opened and a familiar face appeared. It was Priscilla.

'Whit are ye doing back? I thought ye were off tae yer bash?' said the Bumble.

'It was cancelled. Somebody supplied dodgy sandwiches and folk are now either hanging their arses over the lavvy or examining the inside of the bowl.' She took off her purple plastic coat and draped it over the back of the settee revealing a glittering black cat suit.

'We're just going out for a wee while, sweetheart' said the Bumble.

Priscilla turned and said, 'If ye think I'm going tae be stuck in this place on ma oan for the rest of the night you've got another thought coming.'

'But its business we're going out for,' bleated the Bumble.

'Aye, I know what type of business ye get up tae, three guys out on Christmas Eve,' she said.

'It's no like that. We're going tae see about the gold,' said the Bumble apologetically.

I sighed and looked at Charlie who raised an eyebrow and unwrapped another toffee.

'Why did ye not say?' she said, 'I'll come with ye, we don't want any other bastard waltzing off with our assets do we? Besides I fancy a jaunt. Where ye going?'

'Dumbarton,' I said, hoping that would put her off.

'My Auntie Betty lives down there,' she said, 'we could drop in and wish her a Happy Christmas.'

'Look,' I said, 'lets go. And if you come, you stay in the car while we do our business, is that clear?'

She gave me a hard look and picked up her coat.

In the background the crew of the good ship Enterprise were off to explore other cultures and galaxies. We were about to do the same in Dumbarton.

Chapter 22

I sat in the front. The Bumble and the Queen of the Dead were in the back. Charles T. McLeod was in the Captain's seat. Snow had begun to lie and sent us into an occasional slide as the Capri tried to gain traction on the road. I turned round to speak to the Bumble. 'You know Davie, Wilde considers you his partner on the gold angle.'

'Well he can dream on.' He gave Priscilla a reassuring smile and squeezed her hand. Amazing what money can do for your relationship.

'Fair enough,' I said, 'But you can tell him that in person if our paths cross.'

Charlie turned the blower higher for warm air while the wipers cleared the drifting snowflakes.

I found a compilation tape of Tamala Motown numbers in the glove compartment and put it on. The Four Tops began to sing *Its The Same Old Songs.*

Like a social historian the Bumble informed us that his father remembered when the Glasgow gangs used to sing along to this at the Barrowlands dancehall. Only instead of 'the same old songs' they sang 'it's the same old Tongs'.

'Ye know, as in *Tongs ya Bass!*' Nobody said anything. 'The Tongs were a Glasgow gang... nothing to do with the Chinese you understand.'

'We know,' I said.

'Would ye look at that fucking eejit!' Charlie exclaimed, as some sort of four-wheel drive sped past, spraying us with a mixture of snow, slush and grit.

We were a few miles from our destination when Priscilla announced, 'I need a pish.'

I muttered a 'God's strewth! Anybody on our tail?' I said to Charlie.

He checked his rear-view mirror. 'If there is then they're staying well back. There's a Little Chef service station coming up,' he added. 'Want me tae pull in?'

'Yeah,' I said, 'we don't want your upholstery getting soiled.'

A quiet 'fuck you' emanated from behind my seat.

Charlie swung the Capri off the dual carriageway. I got out and pushed the front passenger seat forward to allow Priscilla out. 'Mind,' I said, 'no calls to anyone, not even your Auntie.'

'Think I'll take a leak as well,' said the Bumble and levered himself out the back seat. 'Christ, can ye no' get yerself a decent four door motor, McLeod.' I gave him a hand. He walked crab like for a few paces then straightened up.

Charlie started on another toffee. 'Reckon we'll find anything?' he said, staring into the night.

'I really don't know,' I said.

A couple of minutes later the Bumble and Priscilla reappeared laughing and joking. Charlie ejected the cassette from the stereo and replaced it with Elvis's Christmas Album –

Here Comes Santa Claus, Here Comes Santa Claus, down Santa Claus Lane, announced the King.

Half an hour later we found ourselves in the Bonhill housing estate, Dumbarton. Even with a smattering of snow it looked as bleak as its reputation. A couple of kids throwing snowballs at passing people were good enough to tell us where Keir Hardie Street was. It was slightly amusing and ironic that we were looking for a Nazi in a street that was named after one of the founding fathers of Scottish Socialism.

We drew up outside a block of 1930s built council flats that hadn't seen whitewash since Keir Hardie had been in shorts. An old mattress lay on the snowy bank leading up to the steps towards the entrance to number 110. The ubiquitous supermarket trolley lay on its side next to it.

'This it?' asked Charlie.

'Yeah,' I said, 'I think so.'

An old guy with a dark woollen hat leaned out of a top floor window. He looked down at our arrival and spat.

'Who's going up?' said the Bumble.

I turned round. 'You and me, Santa,' I said. 'Charlie will turn the car round and be waiting in the event we have to get out of here fast and also serve as a lookout for any unwanted guests – along with the love of your life.'

I got out. The Bumble levered his arse up from the back seat. He straightened up beside me and surveyed the territory. The elderly gent looked down and spat again as he watched us. I got out my cigs and offered the Bumble one.

'What are we going tae say tae the guy if he's in?' he said blowing smoke with force through his nose like a factory chimney.

'That we're from the Christmas Awareness Society telling folk that Santa is an anagram of Satan. Let's just...' Before I could finish what I was saying there was a shattering of glass on the frosty pathway.

'What the fuck...' said the Bumble. The old guy cackled loudly and pointed to an open window below where a party seemed to be on the go, judging by the festive dance music.

'I told ye it was fucking Apache country,' said the Bumble taking a deep draw on his cigarette.

'C'mon,' I said and headed towards the entrance. The place stank of pish and the walls were decorated in primitive phallic drawings. There were comments on the performance of Celtic and Rangers football clubs and an insult to the Pope. An anthropologist would have been delighted at the find. I turned round to the Bumble who looked decidedly nervous.

'Are ye sure this is it?' he said. 'Why would an old Nazi live in a doss joint like this?'

'Fuck knows,' I said. 'They didn't all end up with luxurious life styles in South America or Spain. Look at Eichmann. He ended up as a bunny breeder before the Israelis put a rope around his neck.'

As we made our ascent, I noticed that several of the doors were made of steel. A few minutes later we were on the top floor.

'Reckon this it?' wheezed the Bumble, glancing at the blue door on the right side of the landing.

'Aye.'

He took a final puff on his cig. I did the same and flicked the fag down the stairs. Pulling out my wallet I thumbed through a selection of business cards I'd been given over the years. I discounted *Lawrence McKenzie, Sales Executive for*

Rolls Royce cars and *John Moore, Bachelor of Dental Surgery.*
Then settled on the obvious – the man from H.I.A.G. I rapped
the door. There didn't seem as though there was anybody at
home. Then it opened an inch protected by a chain. The old
guy with the blue woolly hat who had watched our approach
peered out. 'Whit dae ye want? Yer no Jehovah's or
something?'

If this was Alfred Kaminski he had done a good job on
losing the foreign accent.

'Merry Christmas,' I said. 'My colleague and I are from the
firm.' I presented the glossy black card with silver embossed
H.I.A.G. on it. He studied it and continued to peer at us.

The dim light from the stairwell made his rough features
look as though they had been carved from a hunk of gnarled
wood. His face resembled a Wooden Indian outside a saloon or
a hardware store in the Wild West. He gave a hacking cough,
spat, and returned the calling card. To my amazement he undid
the chain and pulled the door back.

'Ye had better come in,' he said. 'They said somebody
would be calling.'

I froze and looked at the Bumble who had read my mind.
We had been expected.

'Are ye coming in or no?'

'Aye, right,' I said and stepped in. The Bumble did likewise.

A solitary low-wattage bulb lit the hall, which lacked any
floor covering. He beckoned us. We entered what was a living
room, aware of our footsteps on the bare boards.

An electric coal-effect fire stood on the hearth, a meagre
heat emanating from its single bar. In every corner sat stacks of
empty vodka bottles. Apart from the telly and a budgie in a
cage, the room had little else beyond a blue velour settee, a

couple of worn armchairs and a coffee table that had something large on it covered with a black cloth.

'Jesus!' said the Bumble as he surveyed the room.

The place was bloody brass monkey's. The window I had seen the Wooden Indian leaning out of was still open.

'You'll have a wee drink since it's Christmas Eve, gentlemen?' he said, and disappeared into the kitchenette before waiting for a reply. Not that I was going to turn it down given the temperature.

The Wooden Indian returned with shot glasses that had scenes of Scotland on them and handed us one each. I got the red-leaded girders of the Forth railway bridge. He then bent down and picked up a vodka bottle and poured measures into our glasses and as he did so I noticed little gold flakes suspended in the spirit. He must have noticed my interest. 'It's a special vodka,' he said, 'they call it *Geldwasser*, it's from the Ukraine.'

'Interesting,' I said. 'Do they stock it at Victoria Wines?'

He gave a little smile. 'Unfortunately not.' He raised his glass. 'Tae Saint Nick.'

I raised my own glass and downed the contents in one go. It burned and then a warm glow developed. The Bumble looked apprehensive but did likewise. Instantly our glasses were refilled. Then we heard coughing coming from another room and somebody else spitting. I looked at the Bumble and then the Wooden Indian.

'That'll be Alfred,' he said. 'His lungs are'nae so good these days either. Smokes too many of these.' He held up his hand-rolled cig. I noticed the nicotine brown shade on his fingers. 'I'll gae him your card.' He wandered through to another room and we heard a few quiet words of conversation about ourselves.

A few moments later the Wooden Indian resumed his perch at the window as a familiar, well-dressed elderly gentleman wandered in from the hall.

'I was told we could expect esteemed company,' said the guy I had last seen with the militaria dealer.

Christ, I thought, we've walked in on the Nazi Odd Couple.

Chapter 23

'Good evening gentlemen, may I introduce myself, former *Oberleutnant* Alfred Kaminski.' He was dressed in a blue uniform with silver epaulettes. An Iron Cross was suspended on his neck by a red white and black ribbon. The old comrade had gone for comfort over style and omitted jackboots in favour of green tartan carpet slippers.

He must have been in his eighties at least but he was still a tall and imposing figure with deep-set blue eyes and a sprinkling of white hair. A piece of cigarette paper was stuck to his cheek where he had recently cut himself shaving.

He slowly raised his right arm, '*Heil Hitler!*'

'Aye, er *Heil* and all that,' I said returning the salute. I nudged the Bumble who gave a half hearted salute. 'He's got arthritis in the shoulder, it's the damp weather.'

Sit down gentlemen, forgive our humble abode but circumstances...' Alfred poured himself a *Geldwasser* and raised his glass, 'The Reich.'

I nudged the Bumble again and we muttered, 'The Reich.' This had been easy so far. I got out my cigs and offered them around. The Wooden Indian glanced in my direction, shook his head and spat out into the night air. I wondered if there was anyone else waiting in the wings to introduce themselves.

Alfred shuffled over to the coffee table, and like a stage magician whipped off the black cloth that had been covering the large object.

'Jeeezus fuck!' the Bumble said under his breath. He stared in disbelief. 'It's no made of chocolate is it?' We all looked at a life size bronze bust of Adolf Hitler. I went over and tapped it. The Bumble did the same.

'No it's no' chocolate,' I said, 'It's got the same sound you get when you tap your neck Davie – best brass.'

'It's nae brass!' said the Wooden Indian from his perch by the window. He coughed and spat more phlegm into the night air. I just hoped there wasn't any poor sod standing below looking up for the star in the east. He pulled the blue woollen hat down further over his ears and resumed his watch.

'You had to admire the man,' said Alfred, 'he had some good ideas, a little misunderstood...' He didn't finish the sentence and shrugged his shoulders. 'But that is of little interest to yourselves since you are really outsiders. I know who you both are.'

'You do?' I said.

'Of course.'

'Then you'll know why we are here,' I said.

'For the gold of course,' he said with a relaxed smile.

'You're well informed.'

'Aye,' said the Bumble, 'who the hell told ye we were coming?'

'*Ein klein vogel* my friends – a little bird. They will be here shortly. You've wasted your time though. The gold is not here.' Alfred stepped forward and refilled our glasses.

I politely tapped ash from my cigarette into a bottle blue glass ashtray beside the Führer.

Alfred patted the bust and smiled again. 'You know he disliked smoking intensely. I met him only the once, Christmas Eve 1940. I was decorated with this Iron Cross.' He sighed and raised his glass. 'The Führer!' He downed the drink.

Momentarily, Alfred was in another world, day-dreaming of a past that must have been light years removed from his present circumstances. Christmas I guess brings all sorts of emotions to the surface. I sipped my *Geldwasser* and tried a stab in the dark. 'Did you know Rudolf Hess?

'Yes,' he said snapping out of his trance, 'I knew the Deputy Führer, quite well in fact! We were both flyers, both loved the freedom of the air, the power of an aircraft.' He lifted the bottle of *Geldwasser*, leaned forward and topped up our glasses then his own.

'He feared for our Fatherland you know. He wasn't alone, that's why I flew with him.'

'You flew with him?' I said, 'here? To Scotland.'

Alfred studied Hitler. 'Great man that the Führer was, we could not hope to win by fighting on two major fronts. So, when the Deputy Führer asked me to accompany him I agreed. Great Britain and Germany should never have gone to war.'

'You were on the same plane?' I said. 'Together?'

He sipped his drink and nodded. 'The Messerschmitt 110 was a difficult plane to escape from, you needed to flip it over.' He demonstrated with a movement of his hand. 'I kept the aircraft on a steady course as the Deputy Führer bailed out. Haa! and to think all these years he was credited with such an incredible feat of flight!'

'You would have all been hanged with piano wire if Adolf here found out.'

Alfred nodded. 'Of course, but he too admired this country – just think if we had succeeded!' He started to cough, pain visible on his face. 'We could have vanquished the communist barbarians – no cold war – man could have advanced!'

For a moment I considered arguing with him about the morality of the Third Reich and then took out one of the old black and white photographs that I had found in Edinburgh. It was the one of a young couple. The man was in uniform, a German uniform, while a young girl smiled and linked arms with him. I passed it to Alfred.

'So, who are they?' said the Bumble.

'It was taken in 1939,' answered Alfred with a sad smile as he stared at the photograph. 'I was twenty. The girl was Bettina... she volunteered to leave Germany and come here. She married another agent working for Hess, Peter Van Luben.'

The Bumble attempted to interrupt, but Alfred simply held up his hand and continued to explain. 'Bettina knew that I had been captured during the war so she ended up marrying that criminal, Van Luben, who helped himself to the gold, the gold that I and Deputy Führer Hess brought with us.'

'How did Van Luben get the gold?' I said. 'Your plane was found and no doubt searched.'

Alfred rolled another cigarette. 'It wasn't left in the plane, it had its own parachute attached to the box. It took time for your Home Guard to find me... they were too busy with the Deputy Führer... so I had time to bury it. Later I made the mistake of conveying to Bettina its location in a coded letter... a mistake.'

There was deeper sadness in his voice. Again he studied the old photograph. I struck my Zippo and offered him a light.

'Thank you,' said Alfred and blew out a cloud of smoke, 'I told the authorities as a Pole I had been obliged into fighting for Germany. I told them I had bailed out of another plane that had engine problems and had probably crashed into the Clyde estuary. After the war I started to look for Bettina and found her in Glasgow... married to that traitor Van Luben!'

He sank back into his armchair and took another sip of the gold-flecked vodka.

'Were you going to kill him?'

'Yes,' he said with an air of satisfaction, 'but then I saw how happy Bettina was with Van Luben... she had fallen in love with him.'

'All's fair and that,' quipped the Bumble.

'And she was no longer impressed with you,' I said.

He shook his head. 'No.'

'You know she's dead?'

Alfred nodded. 'I was there when she died.' A heavy silence pervaded the room. 'I went to see her, we ended up arguing, I wanted some compensation... she still had some of the gold.'

'Why wait all these years?'

'Van Luben had powerful friends in Glasgow, dangerous ones who would have not hesitated to kill.'

'That sounds familiar,' I said and gave the Bumble a quick glance.

'Van Luben could only use the gold a little at a time without raising attention to himself... I was a fool in going to see her, she rejected me, pushed me away... she lost her footing on the stairs...'

'It was an accident? Wasn't it?'

Alfred nodded, 'I made an anonymous call to the police.'

'And the documents?' I said, 'where did they fit in?'

Alfred's eyes were watery as he looked across. 'I buried them with the gold in a waterproof cover. The Deputy Führer trusted me. He didn't want to be captured with them. It would have made him look like a common thief.'

He coughed again as he took a draw on his rollup. 'He was a great man helping his country!' Alfred held a handkerchief to his mouth coughing violently into it. 'Look around you, my reward for loyalty to Germany!'

I was beginning to think that Alfred had flown all right – straight over the cuckoo's nest.

The Bumble stood up. 'I've had enough of this, the gold ain't here, c'mon lets go.'

The Wooden Indian produced a black Luger pistol and waved it at him. 'Sit on yer fat arse and shut up.'

The Bumble glared back but decided to do as he was told. 'How much is he paying you bastards?' he said.

Alfred looked puzzled.

'Kev Barr, did he put the pair of you old soap dodgers up tae this?'

Alfred glanced at the Wooden Indian who was still keeping one eye on the Capri down below and another on us.

'I've never heard of the gentleman,' said Alfred.

'There's a big motor coming up,' announced the Wooden Indian with the conviction of a redskin with his ear to the ground.

Chapter 24

I made a move toward the window. The Wooden Indian levelled the Luger.

'Easy on the trigger finger pops, I only want to see who's out there.' I watched the approaching headlights of the car reflect off the snow. It stopped, probably so the occupants could search for the numbers on the flats and then carried on to the top of the road turned and came back down. It drew up behind the Capri. The Wooden Indian rested his pistol on the window ledge. We watched as a familiar female got out and momentarily chatted to Charlie through the Capri window. They both looked up. A second or two later Charlie and Priscilla joined her and headed up the path.

'Mind,' I said, 'no shooting. I know it wouldn't go amiss up here in Bonhill, but let them get inside first.'

He made no reply, merely spitting out the window again. I heard Priscilla shouting. 'Ye filthy old bastard, that could have hit me!'

I looked over at the Bumble. 'Hey, Davie, the love of your life just missed getting gobbed on.'

Unease sat on his face. 'What's she coming in for?'

'Wait and see,' I said. 'She's got company and it isn't just Charlie.'

The Wooden Indian answered the door and ushered the new guests in. The Marmalade Cat appeared followed by Priscilla and Charlie.

'What the Hell are you doing here!' said the Bumble.

Before she could reply the Wooden Indian displayed the hardware in his hand. Mine host Alfred stood up and smiled. 'Welcome.' He noticed the way the Luger was angled at his new guests. 'Please Bernie, be careful with that gun. You'll have to excuse him, he gets enthusiastic about his loyalty.' Alfred straightened himself up as though he was on parade and shuffled the heels of his carpet slippers together. 'Allow me to introduce myself, I'm Alfred Kaminski, former aide and pilot to Rudolf Hess, Deputy Führer of the Third Reich and the greater Fatherland.'

'Nice tae meet a man with manners,' said Priscilla, completely unfazed by the situation.

'Forgive me,' said Alfred opening a chrome cigarette box, offering it to the Marmalade Cat and then Priscilla. 'I keep these for guests.' Alfred lit their cigarettes in turn then sparked up his own hand rolled fag from a pouch of tobacco, took a deep satisfying draw and said, 'I'm an old man with little left, the glory of the past is all I have.'

'Who's the geezer on the table?' said Priscilla. 'Charlie Chaplin?'

I thought Alfred was going to have a stroke. 'Why, that is one of the greatest leaders in world history! That is Adolf Hitler!'

Charlie caught my attention and glanced toward the Wooden Indian. I shook my head. Trying to jump him was too risky with so many people in the room.

'Hey, there's another strange car coming up,' announced the Wooden Indian.

I indicated to him that I wanted to have a look. The large Mercedes drew up in front off the Capri. Another familiar figure stepped out. This was going to be a Christmas Eve to remember.

'That will be our final guest,' said Alfred. 'Bernie the door please.'

The Wooden Indian muttered something under his breath and went out to the hallway.

Alfred lifted the bottle, '*Geldwasser*, my dears?'

'Aye,' said Priscilla, 'dinnae mind if ah do. Is that one oh those alcopops?'

Alfred filled several shot glasses.

'Quite a wee *soiree* you've planned,' said the Bumble holding out his glass for a refill.

Alfred ignored him and handed a glass to the Marmalade Cat. She shivered and pulled her fur coat together for warmth, giving a confident smile in our direction. I listened to the sound of footsteps approaching. Charlie looked ready to make a move again but I shook my head. I wanted to see who our final party goer was.

Then the living room door opened and in stepped Toad of fucking Toad Hall: Aaron Schoenberg.

'Good to see you,' Alfred said, as though we were at a meeting of Nazis Re-united. Schoenberg shook hands with him like an old friend.

'You know each other?' I said

'Yes,' said Alfred, 'I also knew his father quite well.'

The Marmalade Cat moved over to stand beside him. I could see now that it had been a set up. Things were falling into place.

'Just whit the fuck are ye doing with him?' demanded the Bumble.

'Sorry Davie,' she said, 'but I wasn't going to let an idiot like you and that hairy Mary over there walk off with the gold after the fuck up with my money.'

'Who the hell are ye calling a hairy!' shouted Priscilla, 'Yer nothing more than an old slag yerself!' I doubted if anyone in the neighbourhood was concerned at the exchange. Most likely they thought it was just the usual Bonhill Christmas spirit.

'Hey!' shouted the Bumble, 'keep the heid – all of you!'

The warring parties simmered down.

'Okay,' I said, 'since the battle lines have been drawn and folk have declared their intentions, how about some truth round here?'

'Like what?' said the Marmalade Cat taking the lead.

'Like did you kill Tony?'

She knocked back the *Geldwasser.* 'He refused to tell me where the cash was.'

'What are you talking about?' said the Bumble.

'Tony stole that money from me! The same money you were going to keep until that idiot Jim took it! I went to Edinburgh to talk Tony round to handing it back in a nice way.'

'You were also fencing the gold,' I said, 'correct me if I'm wrong.'

'You always were the brains of the outfit,' she said. 'The money was for the last lot I processed for Mrs Van Luben before she died.'

I brought out my fags and lit one without offering them around.

'You seduced Tony,' I said. Nobody stripped him and beat him up. There were no signs of violence in the room when I got there and it was just too kinky a death even for Kev Barr and the Russian. You persuaded him to try the ultimate by cutting off his oxygen supply to heighten the sex.'

'When needs must,' she said. 'He was happy to play along.'

'Jesus up a fucking Christmas tree!' said the Bumble. 'He was your son.'

'Stepson,' she corrected.

'And you tipped off Kev Barr,' I said, 'soon as you heard from Davie that I'd gone to Edinburgh. What were you hoping for? Some mug to take the blame for killing him?'

'One of you was meant to take the rap.' She smiled satisfied with herself. 'But things worked out anyhow.'

'You knew he was dead before I went through to Edinburgh.' I stared at the Bumble. 'Didn't you?'

He went pale and found something interesting on the carpet. 'She told me there had been an accident, not that she'd murdered him... I needed somebody to check it out.'

'And that's where I came in.' I took a draw on my fag.

'But I swear,' said the Bumble, 'that I had nothing to do with Kev Barr turning up.' He looked up. 'Believe me.'

'Your sister also had a little help from the crooked lawyer here.'

The Marmalade Cat moved closer to Schoenberg.

'Naturally,' he said, 'I'd been her business lawyer for years, and Frank McCaffrey's before that. The documents please, I presume you brought them with you?'

'They're back at the flat,' said the Bumble.

'Liar!' The Marmalade Cat brought out a small calibre automatic.

'Hey cum'oan, there's nae need for this,' the Bumble pleaded.

The Wooden Indian levelled his Luger at the Bumble as well for extra measure. Aaron Schoenberg casually lit a cigar and said, 'You came here hoping to do a deal with Alfred here, and the only collateral you have to offer are the documents for the deposit account. I suggest you hand them over before Bernie blows out what little brains you have.'

The Bumble slowly reached inside his coat pocket and withdrew the small green book.

'It was you,' I interjected, 'who put the old newspaper under the carpet at Davies's office and no doubt bribed the Chinaman to point me in your direction, since you knew what was going on.'

'You're a talented man,' said Schoenberg. 'Reuben and I are old friends.'

'Tell me,' I said, 'the night Davie's office went up in flames you drove down ahead of me didn't you? Waited for me to take the bait and then tried to fry me.'

He started to clap. 'Give the man a coconut.'

You're a guy who doesn't like loose ends.'

Schoenberg shrugged his shoulders again. 'Naturally, I'm a lawyer.'

'What about the old guy who lived there? What if he never got out?'

'Sometimes innocents have to suffer,' he said.

'That's fucking rich,' I said, 'you a Jew, and you behave like a Nazi! What am I saying?' I studied Schoenberg and then Alfred. 'You're not a Jew – are you?'

Schoenberg turned to the Marmalade Cat. 'I thought you said he was the brains of the outfit? Allow me to properly introduce myself. Stefan Pasternak.' He smiled again, full of his own arrogance, and tapped ash from his cigar into the ashtray next to the bust of the Führer. 'No I'm not a Jew, but they would be the first to advise you to try and blend in if you want to survive. My father was an SS officer who served with *14th Waffen SS Galizien Division* recruited in the Ukraine. Many were given refuge here after the war to help in the fight against the Communists.'

I felt anger rise to the surface. 'He was a war criminal then?'

'Is the son responsible for the sins of the father?'

'Never mind your old man, guilt is written all over you,' I said, 'and greed.'

'Oh,' he said casually, 'and you lot were going to donate any new found wealth to charity?'

I stepped forward to put out my cigarette, paused for a second and then stubbed it into Hitler's scalp. The bronze unexpectedly sizzled.

'*Die Führer!*' said Alfred.

I thought he was going to burst with rage as he observed the main man being desecrated. Nobody seemed to notice Adolf now had a small gold spot on his scalp.

'Now,' said Schoenberg, 'if we're quite finished please hand over the paperwork for the Swiss account.'

The Bumble reached forward to hand the pass-book to him – the Wooden Indian raised his gun. 'Christ! You've got what you want.'

For a moment or two I really thought he was going to pull the trigger until Schoenberg motioned with his hand to lower the gun.

'And what about you Alfred?' I said. 'Where do you fit into their plans?'

'Once the final funds have been withdrawn I will return to the Fatherland with honour.' Pride swelled up in Alfred. '*Deutschland Uber Alles*!'

There's no fool like an old fool, I thought. I glanced at Charlie and then towards the Wooden Indian, who had his head out of the window for yet another quick gob.

'Linda, we can work this out,' pleaded the Bumble.

'Get real,' she said, her index finger tightening on the trigger of her automatic.

The Wooden Indian started to swing his head back in, but it was too late. Charlie rammed the top section of the sash window down on his neck with a dull thud. He gave out a squawk and a loud crack barked from the Luger.

I half raised my arm for self-protection but by the time I had reacted Schoenberg had taken the bullet. His grey matter stippled the walls. He collapsed beside the fireplace. A reddish slime slowly dribbled down the wallpaper. He lay still on the floor, a gurgling sound bubbling from his mouth. The smell of blood and gunpowder filled the room. Priscilla had the presence of mind to go for the Marmalade Cat, trying to grab her gun. As she did so, there was another crack, and Alfred slumped to the floor.

I looked across at Charlie who had managed to grab the comatose Indian's gun. Alfred was on the floor face down. In the middle of his back a small dark red hole oozed blood. Priscilla calmly took the Marmalade Cat's gun and shoved her down onto the settee. Bending down, I could see Alfred was still breathing. His eyes flickered as I attempted to see how bad the wound was.

'Leave me, please,' he said, 'I am quite happy to die.'

'Hey, come on Pops,' I said, 'its not that bad.' His eyes met mine.

'Please,' he said, attempting a smile, 'scatter my ashes at the airfield... in Augsburg where I began this journey...' He coughed, blood flowed from his mouth. 'Please.' His voice trailed off to a hiss. A few seconds later he went still. I knew he was dead before I felt for the pulse in his neck. I closed his eyelids and took a red tartan travelling rug from his chair and covered him.

Chapter 25

Outside on the landing I could hear shouts and dugs barking, doors getting opened and a woman screaming to someone to send for the Polis. I could also hear Christmas Carols somewhere below and swore I heard a tenor voice singing: '*God rest ye Jerry Mentalmen.*'

A pot pourri of unpleasant aromas pervaded the room.

'What a fucking mess,' said the Bumble surveying the scene. 'What are we going to do now?'

I brought out the mobile and my note book then dialled. 'Wilde? Get yer bloody arse here fast.' I gave him the address, then hung up. I took out some cigs, threw one to the Bumble then lit one for Priscilla and handed it to her. It was then, as I lifted a cig to my mouth, that I noticed how much my hands shook. Nobody said anything. We all just looked at the three bodies, the Führer and the gore.

I went over to the window for a breath of air. Charlie wiped his prints off the Wooden Indian's Luger with the curtains and dropped the gun to the floor beside his limp body. I checked for a heartbeat. He was dead, his neck probably broken. Charlie and I looked out into the night that was Christmas Eve and at the mob that had started to gather below. A few shouted and pointed up.

I took the small automatic from Priscilla, wiped it clean, then placed it in Schoenberg's right hand and squeezed his already cold fingers around it. The Marmalade Cat looked on then lowered her eyes.

We all waited. The singer below offered up *Silent Night... Holy Night*. I filled up the shot glasses with *Geldwasser* and passed them round. Wilde arrived on the scene within minutes, which meant he must have tailed us from Glasgow. The bastard couldn't lose no matter what the outcome. He had simply played the waiting game. Strolling in with his sidekick he gave out a loud whistle. 'Bit of a seasonal shindig on the Huns, wouldn't you say Malkie?'

Malkie, his assistant was turning a greener shade of pale at the sights that greeted him.

'Never seen anybody shot before,' he said running out the door, throwing up as he went.

Wilde looked at Alfred. 'Hope it was'nae our friends turn to clean the landing, otherwise that puke is going to stay there for a wee while. Mind you, round here I don't suppose they'll notice much difference.'

'You're all heart,' I said.

'This the murder weapon here?' Wilde picked up the Luger with a pen through the trigger guard.

'It wasn't murder,' I said, 'it was self defence.'

Wilde raised his eyebrows in mock surprise. 'And you expect me to believe that?'

'I've got a room full of witnesses, haven't I?'

'This lot? They could'nae tell the truth to save their grannies.' He blew his nose with his familiar crusty hanky.

'Believe what you want, but we'll all swear that the old guy in the window shot in self defence. It was all about thieves falling out.'

'So how come his heid is trapped in the window?' asked Wilde.

'He needed a bit of fresh air,' I said. 'Did you know the majority of fatal accidents happen in the home?'

'That's right,' Charlie said. 'Saw it happen... these old windows are a disgrace.'

'I don't suppose you've checked for a pulse?' Wilde said looking at the Wooden Indian.

'He never had one to begin with,' replied Charlie and proceeded to unwrap a toffee. He flicked the silver foil out the window to join the other rubbish piling up below.

Wilde looked round the room eying us all up and down including the Führer. 'Fucking jinxed to the hilt this place,' he said. 'Ye'd better have something for me, like documents of access to a Swiss account, otherwise it's goodnight Vienna and Christmas lunch in the Bar-L for the lot of ye. Except you ladies of course. You'll be off to Corton Vale for a bit of tongue and groove with the dykes. Cum'oan hand them over! Ye've got yerselfs in a hole and I'm the only guy that can get ye out of it... for a price.'

The bastard was enjoying this. 'The documents are with our friend there' said the Bumble and nodded towards Schoenberg.

Wilde glanced at the body, bent down, searched the pockets and found what he was after. 'You're lucky Davie,' very lucky, that I'm feeling seasonal.'

'Are we supposed to be grateful?' I said.

'Listen Sunny Jim, it's the least you can do for me since I got Kev Barr of yer back. Good show at the station for the

Christmas punters, wasn't it?' Wilde smiled right at me. 'Having him picked up like that. Especially when he was on his way up tae let that stupid dug of his have yer dumplings for a seasonal lunch.' Wilde gave a violent sneeze.

On the landing outside I could hear several voices. Malkie was holding back the curious locals.

'We have an understanding then?' Wilde said and headed towards the front door of the flat to check on the situation. 'Remember the nice man here is going to do you all a big favour and let you walk.'

Wilde went to the hallway. 'It's all right folks,' I heard him say, 'this is a Special Branch matter. Our team is on its way. Secure the entrance Malkie and keep those fucking kids back. Oh and if you can find a bucket and mop, you can start to clean up the puke.'

Wilde wandered back into the room as though he was on a visit to his favourite auntie's. 'My team'll be here in about half an hour,' he said, 'maybe more, depends on how many of them are sober.'

He casually picked up my packet of cigs from the table and lit up. He was like the man who had just broken the bank at Monte Carlo. Wilde lifted the slumped remains of Alfred with his toe and then looked at Schoenberg and the gore. 'Always knew he had nae brains.' He laughed then brought out his grimy hanky and gave another loud blow into it.

'You know you should try some alternative medicine for that cold,' I said.

'Like what?' Wilde studied the contents of his hanky like a soothsayer.

'Like Urine Therapy.'

'Urine Therapy? Whit's that?'

'It's the same as you're doing to us,' I said. 'It's called taking the piss.'

He glared at me but I couldn't care less.

'Right you lot,' he said eventually, 'bugger off! Cum'oan beat it! Before I change my mind!'

I flicked my ash over Schoenberg.

'Ye've just sorted out ma retirement fund,' said Wilde, 'and I don't want anyone asking awkward questions. I'll invent something for this lot. Now go on beat it!' He squinted at The Wooden Indian whose body gave a twitch. He wasn't about to get up again, though.

Our gang silently filed out. Priscilla picked up the bottle of *Geldwasser* and with enviable sarcasm wished Wilde a Merry Christmas. I was the last to leave and I turned to Wilde. 'Do me a favour will you? Could I have the bust of Hitler's heid over there as a souvenir?'

'You're sick,' said Wilde. 'Anybody ever tell you that?'

'Frequently,' I said.

'Whit are you? A Neo-Nazi or something?'

I shrugged my shoulders, 'A Christmas present to myself.'

Wilde shook his head. 'You're not right upstairs, you know that? Aye help yerself tae the Führer, if ye want. Christ! I must be getting soft in ma old age.'

I wrapped the bust with the black cloth and lifted it up onto my shoulder with both hands. Charlie stuck his head back round the door and said, 'Are ye coming?' He gave us a look of surprise at seeing me with my load. 'If we're taking souvenirs,' he said, 'then I'll have that poor budgie.' He picked up the cage with the quivering bird inside. 'At least I'll have someone to talk to over Christmas apart from the wife.' We made our way downstairs to the others, pushing through the crowd on the stairs.

The Bumble and Priscilla left with the Marmalade Cat. Charlie eyed up the bundle I had carried down. He opened the Capri door and I dropped my load onto the passenger's footwell. 'Whit the hell have ye got there, anyway?' he said. Snowflakes twinkled in the headlights as we drove away. I revealed the Führer for the second time tonight. 'Have you gone daft? Whit are ye going tae do with that?'

'I'm going to do the same as happened to the real life version,' I said, 'melt it down.'

I got out a penknife from my pocket and scraped the bust, just to confirm my theory. Sure enough it revealed shiny gold underneath the metallic bronze paint. Alfred had obviously kept a little of Hess's stash for himself. Charlie and I looked at each other and smiled. Reaching forward, I picked up one of his cassettes and pushed it into the stereo. Then I sat back and whacked up the volume as the Shankhill Boyz Band belted out the re-mix version of *The Sash*.

⁋

Printed in the United Kingdom
by Lightning Source UK Ltd.
135873UK00002B/93/P